Maggie was born and grew up in England, and has lived in Canada for most of her life. Now retired she makes her home in a small town in northern British Columbia.

To the Grandfathers

Maggie Carew

Separate Ways

For the other grand daughter
with love

Maggie Carew

AUSTIN MACAULEY PUBLISHERS™

LONDON • CAMBRIDGE • NEW YORK • SHARJAH

A CIP catalogue record for this title is available from the British Library.

ISBN 9781398463530 (Paperback)
ISBN 9781398463547 (ePub e-book)

www.austinmacauley.com

First Published 2022
Austin Macauley Publishers Ltd®
1 Canada Square
Canary Wharf
London
E14 5AA

Thanks are due to my editor, Paul Glover, to Helen Rossum, who taught me all I know (but by no means all she knows) about spinning and weaving, to Jock Mackenzie and the Hazelton Free Range Writers, and to my dear friend Patricia, who taught me to respect spiders.

Preface

A grey granite town on the shore of a grey northern sea, under a heavy grey sky. Facing the sea, a row of grey granite houses with roofs of black slate. Not a tree or a blade of grass to be seen.

Two young men were walking along the waterfront. Alec had freckles and bright red curly hair, the only touch of color in that somber scene. Roger's hair was black, cropped short, and covered with a grey cloth cap. They trudged along the cobbled roadway; hands thrust deep in pockets, shoulders hunched against the wind blowing off the firth, even now in early summer. They were about the same age, had known each other all their lives, had struggled through the limited education offered by the local school, attended kirk on Sundays as much to please their parents as to please God. Now they were very close to abandoning their search for jobs.

"The herring fishery is in bad shape," said Alec, "and the boats are not hiring. Cod fishing is two months away."

"That just leaves the mines," said Roger. "I will not go down the mines – not after what happened to my pa."

Alec sighed. "It seems we have two choices: Leave or starve."

"I don't want to leave Ma," said Roger.

"But if you stay, she'll stay along with you," said Alec. "My granddad left me some money in his will," he told Roger. "I'm thinking of spending it on a ticket to Canada. They tell me there's plenty of work there."

"You're lucky," said his friend. "I can't afford the fare. But I thought I might go south to England."

Alec was horrified.

"You can't go to sassenach country!" he said. "That's where bad people go when they die."

"Here is where the dead go," said Roger, grimly.

Chapter 1
Roger Sets Out

"So goodbye, Ma," said Roger. "I'm away now."

"Have you got everything?" asked Cathy, trying bravely to keep her voice from trembling.

"Here, I packed your dinner. It's not much, I'm afraid. Are you sure about this, son?"

"I mean to try, Ma. I can always come home if I can't find work in England."

He shouldered his knapsack, buckled his money belt securely around his waist, opened the door, squinted up at the rain-threatening sky. He put his arm around his mother's shoulders and kissed her cheek.

"Take care of yourself, Ma," he said, "I'll write."

"Go with my blessing," said Cathy, "and with the blessing of the Lord." Holding back her tears and wringing her hands in her apron.

He took a last look around the familiar room, the only home he had ever known. The furniture was shabby now, but still lovingly polished and cared for. The willow-pattern plates arranged on the dresser, the eight-day clock on the mantelpiece, and the copper kettle on the hob over the fire. He raised his eyes to the heavy oil lamp hanging from the ceiling beam.

"How will you reach to light the lamp?" he asked.

"I'll stand on a chair," she said. "Don't worry about me, son. I'll manage."

He thought how odd it was that she seemed ageless all the time he was growing up, and now suddenly he noticed for the first time that her cheek was soft and powdery, her eyes faded, her lips thin and pale. He felt a pang of guilt at leaving her, but reminded himself that if he couldn't find work soon, they might both starve together. They did not own the cottage and the landlord could turn them out into the street if the rent was not paid. The thought of his beloved mother in the parish workhouse appalled him.

Roger stepped out firmly. He thought, *First steps on a journey.*

At the corner, he looked back. His mother was still standing at the door. He grinned and waved. Then he turned the corner and was lost to her sight.

"If I put a good foot under me," he thought, "I can be in the next village by noon. I can eat my packed dinner and wash it down with a pint at the local pub." Then a second thought, *Better not to spend my money on ale. It looks like rain. I won't want to sleep under a haystack this night.*

"Well… Maybe a pint just this once, seeing as how it's the first day."

As he tramped along the road he soon fell into an easy rhythm and felt as if he could keep up his pace all day. A laden cart plodded by going in the other direction and the carter saluted him. No one he knew.

"Foreign travel already," he thought, "Not just a journey – an adventure."

All his life, as far back as he could remember, he had wakened in the morning knowing what to expect all day, but on this day, he couldn't even predict where he would spend the night, and tomorrow he would be in strange country among strange people on the first of many such morrows. It was a little frightening, but exciting too. He began to whistle, an old folk song, a good walking tune:

Step we gaily, on we go, heel to heel and toe to toe.
Arm in arm and on we go, all for Marie's wedding.

The rain held off. He covered more than twenty miles that day, but as the long summer afternoon dimmed towards dusk, even young Roger grew weary, and his feet ached. He was glad to see the roofs of a village in the distance, and he limped into it as the sun was setting. The village was little more than a widening in the road, stone cottages on each side, a small church perched on a hill, and a pub in the center, the Cat and Pigeons. He went in.

They're not the strangers, he thought. *I'm the stranger.* Stranger indeed!

"Good evening," he said, as heartily as he could manage.

No one answered. Through the silence he made his way to the bar.

"I'd like a pint please, and what can you give me to eat?"

"You can have bread and cheese," said the gruff landlord, "or you can have cheese and bread. Take your pick."

It was good cheese, and good bread, and good ale. He ate and drank with relish and felt much stronger for it. An older man was staring hard at him.

"You looking for work?" he asked.

"Yes, I am," answered Roger. "Are you offering?"

"Ever been to sea?"

"No, never. I've often wondered what that must be like."

"Well, you're young and strong. You might be useful," said the man.

Slowly the other men sitting around his table got up and came to stand around Roger.

"Come with us. You're just the sort we need."

The hair on Roger's nape began to prickle.

"No thanks," he said. "That's not really the kind of work I had in mind. Anyway, time I was just leaving."

Roger had heard of press gangs. They abducted young men to serve on the ships of the Royal Navy in appalling conditions and sometimes in great danger. It was a kind of slavery. He hurriedly drained his mug of ale and in the bottom of it there was a silver coin. He made to stand up and at once there was a firm grip on each of his shoulders.

"Let go of me," he growled between his teeth.

The leader just grinned.

"You took the king's shilling," he crowed. "You are now officially an able seaman in his majesty's navy."

"I did not take your shilling!" protested Roger. "I never touched it."

"The shilling is in the mug, and the mug is in your hands," leered the leader. "And it's not my shilling; it's the king's shilling. You are now legally an able seaman in his majesty's navy. Now you must come with us."

Roger looked around wildly. The other customers were all carefully looking anywhere but at him, noses in pint pots, minding their own business. The men hustled him outside, where they had a cart waiting. As they dragged him towards it, he dug in his heels and struggled hard to escape their grip. Then a sharp pain on the back of his head and – darkness.

When he awoke, with a fierce ache in the back of his head, he found his wrists were bound to one of the staves in the side of the cart. He was gagged. A lump of coarse cloth was stuffed into his mouth and secured by a tight bandage. The cart jolted roughly on the road and a tarpaulin cover blocked out light and sight. Roger began to sweat, limp with fear. How could he have been so stupid.? His first day out in the wide world, fallen victim to a press gang. No bright adventures, no future, no returning home triumphant and rich. He thought about his poor mother waiting, never knowing what had become of him. He wished he had spent more time at the kirk, as Ma had hoped he would. He tried to remember some of the prayers, but what came to mind was the words of a psalm:

...though I walk through the valley of the shadow of death, I will fear no evil, for thou art with me.

Lord *are* you with me? I need you now.

The cart came to a halt. Men's voices, muffled by the tarpaulin so that he couldn't hear what they were saying. Footsteps, moving away. Silence. Roger wept.

Presently he heard footsteps drawing near, just one person by the sound of it. A corner of the tarpaulin was lifted. A rough voice.

"Are you all right son?"

A lantern was shedding a pail beam on him.

"God Almighty, look at the state of you!"

The tarpaulin was dragged away. Roger now saw the silhouette of a man and the glint of a knife in the lantern light.

He's going to kill me! No, no that's not right. Why would he do that? The navy wouldn't pay for a corpse.

The stranger cut easily through the rope that bound his wrists. Roger fumbled with stiffened fingers at the knot of the gag and managed to free himself from it.

"Thank you, oh thank you, sir," he stammered. "I was so afraid."

"Of course, you were," said his rescuer. "Now, can you get up? Let me help you. That's right. Try to walk a bit. Lean on me."

Slowly the numbness ebbed away and Roger was able to stand upright.

"Good. That's good. Now run for it, boy. And God go with you."

"How can I thank you?" asked Roger.

"No need. I have sons of my own. Now go! go!"

Roger hobbled away into the darkness, gaining speed and agility as the stiffness wore off, running as fast and as far as he possibly could. At last, out of breath, he slowed to a steady walking pace. He thought of Alec who had set off shortly before him. But Alec had gone west, towards the sea. Where was he now, he wondered, and what was happening to him?

Chapter 2
Alec Goes West

Alec stepped out firmly, heading west, the morning sun behind him, casting a long shadow before him.

He thought: "The first steps of my journey. New places to see, new people to meet. I don't know what this day will bring, or where I'll spend the night. I have the money for my ship passage, but not much more. I need to be careful about what I spend on the way. Food is more important than comfort, and it's summer, so I should be able to sleep out of doors on most nights. Perhaps I can sleep in barns. Perhaps some farmer will let me work for my supper, perhaps…not to know is a bit frightening, but it's exciting too."

He became aware of being followed and looking behind him he saw a big black dog with amber eyes. It was just padding along, not threatening in any way, but not playful either.

"You look more like a wolf than a dog," said Alec. "Who do you belong to?"

He reached out a tentative hand and let the animal sniff at it.

"No collar? Are you a stray? You can come along with me if you like. I'll be glad of the company."

The dog wagged his tail.

They strode along together, companionably. Alec felt a bit braver with the dog beside him, and so they continued for some miles, until the sun was high overhead. Alec found an ancient oak tree growing by the side of the road, and settled himself comfortably in its shade. He swigged from his leather bottle of beer, and then poured a little of it into his cupped hand and offered it to the dog, who lapped it greedily. In his pack were bread and cheese and a chunk of stewed mutton wrapped in oiled paper. These too he shared with his new friend.

A little further on they found a shallow stream forded by a row of flat stones. Alec took off his boots and waded across, enjoying the coolness of the water on his tired feet. The dog splashed across and shook himself dry on the further bank.

"If we're going to be friends, I should know your name," said Alec. "What should I call you, dog? Jog? Log? Mog?"

The dog seemed to nod his head.

"Mog? Is that what you want me to call you?"

Another nod.

"I do believe you understand every word I say, don't you?"

A long look from the dog's amber eyes.

Alec got his feet.

"Come on, then, Mog my friend. Let's see how far we can go before nightfall."

The weather was warm but not hot. The sky was overcast, promising rain later. A light breeze fanned Alec's face. High overhead a skylark poured out his glorious song.

"It's good to be alive on such a perfect day!" exclaimed Alec.

After a while they found the road had dwindled to a mere cart track and entered a wood. The green shade felt welcoming. There were soft rustling sounds in the dense undergrowth. A small bird perched on a branch at Alec's eye level. It stared hard at him with its bright eye, its head tilted to one side, and chirped a single shrill sound.

"And a good day to you, too," laughed Alec.

As he went on the forest grew thicker and darker, but there was a trail of sorts, a narrow ribbon of leaf mulch bordered by moss, fungi, bracken and a few straggling bushes. But eventually even those were left behind. The hardwood trees gradually gave way to conifers, dense pines and firs, crowding each other, with no ground cover, just earth and needles and the corpses of dead trees. No birds sang here. There was a deep silence except the sound of his own breathing, and furtive rustlings in the undergrowth. He felt as if he was being watched. Clearly he had strayed off the road. He looked around nervously, seeing no movement. He tried to remember at what point the highway had dwindled to this rough trail, but it seemed to have happened so gradually that he had hardly noticed. At that point he might have turned back if not for staunch Mog plodding along patiently ahead of him.

A movement caught the corner of his eye. Just a shiver of leaves, but then as he turned towards it a man leapt out in front of him, a tall, gaunt man in a worn leather coat, unshaven and long haired, grinning through black teeth. Alec cried out. He turned to run but there was another man behind him now. More of them emerged from the bush, all big, dirty and grinning, all holding long knives.

The first man said something in a harsh dialect that Alec did not understand, but he caught a word that sounded like 'luck' and another like 'money'.

"How dare you threaten me!" cried Alec in a tone that he hoped sounded fearless. "I am a wayfarer, passing through your domain. I mean you no harm. Let me pass."

The man behind him seized him and held him tightly with his arms pinned behind him, while the one in front reached for Alec's money belt. His eyes lit up when he saw the cash inside it, that precious bequest that was to pay for the voyage to the new world and a new life. He held up the money to show the others, and then counted it carefully. Then he grabbed Alec's jacket and held him with one hand – the hand with the money in it – and with the other he pointed his long knife at Alec's throat.

Alec feared that he was going to die. He looked around desperately. Where was Mog? Had he deserted him just when a big dog might have been useful? *I'm too young to die*, he thought. *I have a whole life ahead of me God help me.*

Then the man nodded to the one behind. A sudden sharp blow, and the darkness.

When he opened his eyes, Alec saw thin shafts of sunlight piercing the leaves. He could not tell how long he had lain there, perhaps a whole day, perhaps a brief time. He got to his feet slowly and carefully, surprised and relieved to find that he was not bleeding or in pain. Mog was lying beside him, and now he stood up too and stretched. There was no sign of the bandits, or of his money belt. He had no idea where he was, or how he had strayed so far out his way.

So much for my great adventure, he thought ruefully. "What am I going to do now? What on earth am I going to do,

Mog? Where were you when I needed you? Well, at least I'm alive. They might have murdered me. Lead me, Mog. You seem to have more sense than I do. You're a good friend, and I will follow you."

Mog give him a long look out of his amber eyes.

So, on they went together, the dog now leading the way. Gradually they emerged from the deepest part of the forest. Sunlight dappled the leaves of alder and oak and beech. There were ferns and mosses again. The bushes were shedding their blossoms to reveal the small green beginnings of ripe berries. Not yet ready to eat, but it didn't matter. Alec was pleased and surprised to realize that he felt no hunger or thirst and, best of all, nothing hurt.

Chapter 3
Help

Roger made his painful way to the next village, where he found an apothecary's shop with a light still burning in the window. He pushed open the door and went in. A shriveled old man was sitting at the counter. A wall of shelves was behind him, crammed with bottles and jars.

"Love potion?" he asked, looking at Roger with a bored expression over his half-moon spectacles.

"Er, no thank you," said Roger, "I've been hurt. Can you patch me up and maybe give me something for the pain? I should tell you, I was beaten and robbed. I have no money left."

"And you expect me to treat you for free?"

"I'll pay you as soon as I can," replied Roger desperately. "I'll sign a note. I'll work for you. Whatever you wish. But for the Lord's sake, I need some help."

The apothecary stood up; he scarcely reached Roger's shoulder. He stared intently into his eyes.

"Press gang, was it? You'd better sit down," he said.

Roger sat. Skillful but not very gentle fingers felt his scalp and probed his ribs.

"Nasty bruise here," he muttered. "Drew blood from your head. Eyes not dilated though. Wait here."

He shuffled into the back room and emerged with a bowl of hot water and a towel.

"First things first," he said. "There's salt in the water so it may sting a bit. Nothing like salt for cleaning and healing."

He dabbed at Roger's scalp wound and made him wince.

"It's not deep," said the apothecary. "You were lucky."

"I don't feel lucky," returned Roger.

"You got away from them, didn't you? Better without a bandage, I think. Let the air get to it.

"Now let's have a look at your ribs."

Roger opens his shirt.

"Hmm, nasty," murmured the old man. "Does this hurt?"

"Ow, yes!"

"Not broken, though; just bruised. I have something will help."

He rummaged behind the counter and produced an earthenware pot which contained a thick yellow ointment with a clean, out-of-doors kind of smell. He smeared some of it on Roger's ribs.

"Arnica," he said.

Roger was surprised. "What? That little yellow flower that grows so abundantly?"

"The very same."

"I thought, it was a weed."

"Many so-called weeds have virtue," replied the apothecary. "This is one. Now for your pain. Drink this. It's bitter, but it works."

Roger took a deep breath and swallowed the contents of the mug. He grimaced.

"Yuck! What's that stuff?"

"The inner bark of a willow tree. It will soothe the pain, but it will also make you drowsy. Come and lie down in the back room."

He led the way into a tiny, immaculately clean room which had a narrow cot on one wall.

"Lie down," commanded the apothecary.

Roger did as he was told and fell at once into an exhausted sleep. He awoke to sunlight streaming through the window and the gentle domestic sounds of kettle and cups, and the fragrance of tea. The old man looked up from his tasks and smiled.

"Good morning," he said. "Did you sleep well?"

"Wonderfully, thank you," said Roger. "How long did I sleep?"

"Long enough. How do you feel now?"

"I feel well," said Roger, surprised and pleased. "The pain's gone completely."

"Good," nodded the apothecary. "You're young and strong, you see. I've made tea."

"You've been so kind," said Roger, accepting the mug of tea gratefully. "How can I repay you?"

"Well, you know," answered the apothecary with a twinkle in his eyes. "I've been thinking about that. The kind of work I do has no use for unskilled labor. And then, I thought that taking care of you has made me feel good. That's payment itself."

"Yes, but…"

"Off you go, and when you're prosperous come and visit me again. I'm getting old. Perhaps by then there will be something I need."

So, Roger shouldered his pack and strode away, turning once to wave farewell and calling down blessings on the old man.

Chapter 4
Mrs. Tickle

Now through a gap in the trees, Alec saw a clearing and as he emerged into it, he saw that there was a cottage, with a roof of moss-covered thatch and a thin column of blue smoke rising from the twisted chimney. A tethered goat browsed nearby and a black cat reclining before the door stood up and arched her back at the sight of Mog.

A woman came out from behind the cottage. She was tall and white–haired, her wrinkled face worn by time and weather. In each hand she carried a wooden pail full of water.

"And who may you be?" she asked Alec.

"My name's Alec. Good morrow, madam."

She laughed.

"Madam? Nay, lad, I'm no fine lady. You may call me Mrs. Tickle. You are on a journey."

She said it is a statement, not a question.

"Er, yes, I am."

"And you need a place to spend this night."

"Yes, if you please."

"Well, you can earn it, and you may sleep in the shed with the goat."

"Willingly," said Alec. "Let me begin by carrying those pails. They must be heavy for you."

Mrs. Tickle laughed again.

"No heavier than they were yesterday," she said. "I am strong. But you can carry them for me. One into the house, the other to the barn. And pour some into the trough for the goat."

"Would you like me to milk the goat next?" asked Alec.

Mrs. Tickle shook her head.

"She wouldn't let you, lad. She is very particular about that. I will milk Amalthea and you may feed the hens and collect the eggs. Their feed is in the bin. Put the eggs in the wire basket hanging behind the door. You may as well shut them up in the coop for the night. Be sure to latch the door firmly to keep out the foxes."

Alec had never done this before, but he thought it couldn't be very hard. As he stepped into the coop, he felt the gentle atmosphere of the place and a slightly sour but not unpleasant smell. He scooped out a bowlful of the grain in the bin and the hens all came flocking around him. They made gentle clucking noises that added to the restful feeling. He took down the wire basket and groped in the straw of the first nesting box. He found two eggs and placed them carefully in the basket.

But suddenly things were not quite so peaceful. With an angry squawk and a flurry of feathers the rooster attacked, pecking and clawing at Alec's legs. Alec kicked out at him and almost lost his balance The rooster was not deterred. His job was to protect the flock. When Alec reached into the second box, one of the hens pecked viciously at his hand. The others joined in and he was surrounded by beaks and claws and angry voices. Earning his supper would be harder than he thought. But then he heard a low growl and the chickens all froze. Mog stood in the doorway, head lowered, hackles bristling.

"Don't hurt them," cried Alec. "Just get them off me."

With the assured authority of a herd dog, Mog shepherded the rooster and all his wives into the corner of the coop furthest from the row of nest boxes, and held them there while Alec hastily gathered up the rest of the eggs. He backed carefully to the door. In one swift bound, Mog was through the door. Alec closed it firmly and breathed a sigh of relief.

"Thank you, my friend," he said to the dog. "I couldn't have done that without you. I only wish you had been just as protective when the bandits attacked me."

The woman was standing with her hands on her hips, laughing heartily.

"Well done, both of you," she said. "That dog of yours earned his super too. The cat doesn't like him, but no matter. Come into the house, Alec. You too, Mog."

Alec was sure he had not called the dog by name.

"How did you know his name is Mog?" he asked.

She gave him an odd look.

"What else would it be?" she replied.

With that gnomic remark she led the way into the cottage. The room had a dirt floor beaten hard over time. A spacious fieldstone fireplace filled the whole of the end wall. A big iron pot hanging over the glowing logs gave off a rich aroma. There was bread on the table and an earthenware pitcher of beer. She poured some into a mug for Alec, then ladled out a generous bowlful of the stew from the iron pot. A second bowl she set by the fire for Mog, and also a dish of beer. He lapped it with relish.

"Never knew a dog didn't like beer," she said, as she settled herself companionably on the opposite side of the table.

"Gifts of the gods," she said, making a gesture over the food. "Thanks, and praise."

Alec was surprised by this. The gods? Not the Lord? But he held in peace.

They sat in silence, Alec ate merely out of politeness because he still felt no hunger, even though the smell of the stew was delicious.

He became aware that she was observing him closely. He was facing the small window; her face was in shadow.

"I didn't feel hungry or thirsty or tired until just now. I wondered about that. But now with the sight of the food and the good smell of it I seem to remember hunger. Does that make sense to you?"

"Oh, yes," she said, "Here in this place everything is to be experienced almost as though for the first time. This place is…apart. A sort of preparing."

"Preparing for what?"

Mrs. Tickle just smiled. "When you are journeying," she said, "you must be prepared for anything."

"Indeed," laughed Alec ruefully. "I learned that yesterday."

"Whither are you going?" she asked at last.

"West," said Alec.

"Where west?"

"Wherever there is work, and a place to bide." She nodded.

"I think you may find work, and certainly a placed to bide. I'll show you where you can sleep."

It was not quite dark this summer night, but she took up a lantern and lit it from the fire with a spill of straw. Holding it high she led him back across the yard to the barn, and showed him the ladder to the loft.

"I'll not leave the lantern. There's hay up there," she said.

Alec climbed into the loft and was surprised to see Mog stretching himself out at the foot of the ladder.

"Sleep well," said Mrs. Tickle, "and wake when you will. The night noises here are not like those of town, but there is naught can harm you."

With that she left him, and he stretched himself gratefully in the fragrant hay. As he drifted off to sleep, he heard the bark of the fox, and the hooting of a hunting owl. He woke to the rooster's triumphant greeting to the sun. It was already daylight, and gentle clucking sounds told him the hens were already in the yard. He clattered down the ladder and out in to the warm golden morning. Mog was waiting for him and so was Mrs. Tickle.

"Here is bread and water for your journey," she said. "Go now with the blessing of the gods. You will meet many strange folks on your journey, but know that none of them has power to do you harm. Blessings on you, too, Mog."

Mog bowed his head before turning away and leading Alec back to the trail. Mrs. Tickle stood in her doorway watching them go, as the cat rubbed his head against her skirt.

"Going west. He doesn't know yet," she murmured. "I wonder how long before he understands what is happening to him."

Chapter 5
A Meeting on the Road

Roger walked for most of the day. As the sky began to grow darker, he picked up his pace again, but he was tired and hungry and still in pain from the rope burns on his wrists and the ache in his head. The press gang had taken all his money and his few possessions, but at least he was still alive, and free. The road crossed a stream by means of a wooden bridge, and he was able to scramble down the bank. He drank thirstily and washed his hands and face, dunking his head into the water. It was tingling cold and refreshed him, so he continued on his way. "Just little further," he told himself. "If I don't find an inn or a village soon – or even just a haystack – I'll lie down beside the road and sleep as well as I may. It will be dark soon, even at this time of the year, but someone must come along this road, sooner or later."

He had not gone much further when he heard hoof beats behind him. Not a rider, but a slow heavy horse, drawing a wheeled vehicle. The horse was a handsome bay mare, well cared for. So was the wagon, made from polished wood, high-wheeled and ornamented with bright brass. A man in a slouched hat was driving and beside him sat a soberly dressed woman. They were both in their middle years, prosperous in appearance. Roger held up his hand.

"Good morrow," he called. "Can you tell me how far to the next village or town?"

"You on the tramp?" asked the man, though not unfriendly.

"Why, yes," answered Roger, "I'm looking for work."

"What kind of work?" asked the man.

"Anything that will feed me," said Roger.

"What can you do?"

"I have no skills," returned Roger, "but I'm strong and willing to learn."

"Then we are well met," said the man, and he smiled. "Jumped in the back, young man. I was at the hiring fair looking for an apprentice, but all the young men I found there knew everything already. There's no teaching the likes of them. How would you like to learn the weaver's trade?"

"I think I should like that very much," said Roger, and he grinned.

"You have a nice smile," said the woman. "An honest face, I think. What is your name?"

Roger told her.

"Then welcome, Roger. I am Sarah, and my man is Simon – Mr. Webster to you. Are you hungry?"

"Yes, indeed."

"There's a basket in the back there with food and ale. Help yourself."

"How kind you are!" exclaimed Roger.

"Nonsense. A hungry apprentice cannot learn or work."

When they came to the town, Roger was pleased to see that it looked very prosperous and well cared for. The wide cobbled main street opened into a square surrounded by substantial granite buildings: a church, a school, a town hall and a library, their facades brightened by window boxes. Simon steered the wagon on to a side street at the end of which stood fine large house with a high gable. At one side of it stood a barn, and he drove the wagon into it.

"Have you worked with horses?" he asked Roger, who had to admit that he had not.

"I'll show you. Then this will be your job. You unhitch her so, d'ye see, then lead her so into her stall. Always remember to thank her. Her name's Daisy, by the way, and she has been a good friend to us for many a year. Haven't you, Daisy, old girl?"

The huge horse nuzzled his shoulder very gently.

"Now you rubs her down – like this'd ye see? You can do this now. That's right. Good. When you're finished, make sure her manger's full. Feed is in this bin. Make sure you put the lid on tight, else she'll nudge it off and eat too much. Fill up her water trough. Bucket's by the pump in the yard. When you've done all that, close the barn door and come into the house by the back."

"And take your boots off," added Sarah.

Left alone, Roger did as he was told, as carefully and as thoroughly as he possibly could. He was very lucky to have met such good people, he told himself. Like most big draft horses, Daisy was gentle and seemed to understand that she filled up a lot of space. When Roger solemnly bade her goodnight, she nuzzled him as though she was saying thank you.

Roger dutifully took off his boots in the back porch and entered Sarah's immaculate kitchen, where a plain, hearty supper was already spread upon the table. The three of them spent the evening comfortably before a cheerful fire. The Websters asked Roger about himself, and he found himself telling them freely about his growing up in the dull little town, about trying without success to find work, and about leaving at last with his mother's blessing. He told them about his escape from the press gang, and the apothecary who had cared for him even though his money had been stolen.

Sarah and Simon listened with sympathy. At last, Simon took a candle and led him upstairs to a tiny room furnished with a narrow bed, a deal dresser and a rag rug.

"I'll bid ye good night, lad," said Simon. "Hope ye'll be comfortable, sleep well and be up betimes in the morning. I'll leave the candle."

Roger had barely enough time to undress, blow out the candle, and struggle under the patchwork quilt before he fell into a deep sleep.

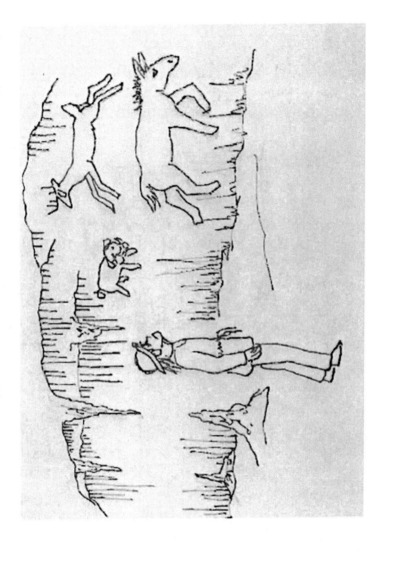

Chapter 6
Trial by Earth and Air

After his sound sleep in Mrs. Tickle's barn, Alec felt refreshed. He strode forward happily, whistling a tune. The track led cross a board expanse of meadowland, spangled with flowers. High overhead a lark poured out his joyful song.

"It's good to be alive." laughed Alec.

Mog made a sound that might have been a cough.

"I could walk for days in this country, in this weather. I have lost track of the days, but no matter. Soon I shall reach the ocean, and then I shall find a ship to take me over it. But I expected a road, a busy highway with much traffic to the seaport. I lost my way completely in that horrible forest. So, I shall just keep heading towards the sunset and once I reach the shore, I can ask for directions. I haven't seen any villages or towns, or even a lonely inn. But as long as this mild weather holds, I can sleep under the stars.

"And I have felt no hunger. Strange that. What about you, Mog? Aren't you hungry? I suppose you can catch a rabbit if you need to. Then you can share with me. After all, I shared with you.

"So let us put a swift foot – or six – under us."

He strode jauntily, whistling, swinging his arms, enjoying the movement, feeling fine. He came to another small farmstead, neat and prosperous looking. The homely sounds of cows and chickens came to him on the gentle breeze, the clanking of pails, a rooster crowing to tell the world what it already knew, for the morning was well advanced. Someone else was whistling too.

There was something odd about the farm. The cottage and the byre were built of rough fieldstone, with roofs of turf that had saplings growing out of it. The fences were of tree branches with thinner branches woven into them. Three cows wandered towards him, curious as cows always are, though not in the least aggressive. They were old-fashioned cows, smaller than most breeds, with coarse brown coats. The hens wandering freely in the yard were small and black.

Then he caught sight of the person who was doing the whistling, a middle-aged man emerging from the byre. He was dressed in breeches and a shirt of coarsely woven cloth, and he wore not a jacket but a sort of tunic of leather. His hair and beard were long and unkempt. He stopped and stared at Alec as though he had never seen a stranger before.

"Good morning to you," called Alec. "It's a fine day."

"Ah," said the man.

"I've come a long way. May I rest here a while and perhaps I could beg a drink of water?"

"Ah," said the man. He turned towards the house and shouted something Alec didn't quite catch. A woman emerged. She too was dressed oddly, in a long gown of the same rough fabric as the man's shirt, and a cloth like a short veil on her head.

The man said something else to her. She nodded, glancing at Alec, and walked to the well at the far side of the yard. It was an old kind of well, with a shingled roof and a windlass with a crank handle and a hook on the end of a rope. She beckoned to Alec to follow her. There was a leather pail of water standing on the ledge of the well. She filled a dipper and offered it to him. He drank gratefully. The water was sweet, and warmed slightly by the morning sun. When he handed the dipper back to her and thanked her, she smiled briefly and returned at once the house.

There was a bench along the sunny house wall.

"May I sit here for a while?" asked Alec.

"Ah," said the man.

So, he sat quietly, enjoying the sunshine on his upturned face, watching the man with interest. For his part the farmer ignored him, busily getting on with his chores. Alec had grown up in a town, even if it was only a small town. He was not familiar with country life or farm tools, but he could tell that the scene before him was old-fashioned, almost everything made by the farmer himself: leather buckets, wattle fences, sod roofs. It felts as though he had strayed out of time. He sat for an hour or so, as nearly as he could judge. Then he stood up and stretched.

"Well, I think I should get on," he said. "Thank you for your kindness, and please thank your lady for me."

"Ah," said the man.

Alec strode out now across the open fields behind the little homestead. The grass was strewn with wild flowers of many varieties, prunella and daisies and buttercups. Bright butterflies fluttered among them. The air smelled sweet and there were many birds: swallows darting after flies and somewhere too high to be seen a skylark sang tirelessly

But his carefree mood did not last.

In the distance he saw a line, or a wall, obscured by haze, hard to make out. It took a long time to draw close enough to see that it was a great cliff, white limestone, sheer and featureless, towering above him and stretching away as far as he could see on either side. There was no other feature in the landscape; no trees, no river; not even meadowland. Alec stared at the cliff with dismay.

"Now what?" he said aloud. "Mrs. Tickle never mentioned this barrier. I shall have to walk all the way around it, and God knows how far out of my way that will take me. And in which direction, I wonder? Left or right, Mog? You choose."

And Mog did. Without hesitation he set off towards their right, towards the north. *So be it,* thought Alec. "It all suddenly seems too hopeless. But it's very odd – I still feel no hunger or thirst and it must be hours since I left Mrs. Tickle. Yet the sun is still behind me and doesn't seem to have moved much higher. As though there was no time passing.

"What is happening to me?" he cried aloud, and his cry echoed raggedly off the face of the cliff.

He was ready to give up in despair, to sink upon the hard barren ground and weep; to turn about, make his way home and start over again. Just then, Mog nudged him and pushed his nose gently against his shoulder. He made a soft sound which was not quite a bark, the sound Alec had come to recognize as a kind of word meaning "look here, pay attention" it was then that he saw the dark patch in the blank cliff face and realized that it was a hole. A doorway, a cave?

Mog walked purposefully into it and Alec followed. Deeper into the cave the daylight of the entrance faded. It should have been completely dark, but he found that he could see well enough. The ground underfoot was clear of obstacles and the walls were smooth. He realized that he was in not a natural cave but a tunnel. Perhaps it would take him through the cliff and out the other side. Everything was so strange that he no longer marveled or questioned but simply accepted, numbly. He followed Mog. He had no sense of time, or distance or even of tiredness. He tried to count his footsteps but kept forgetting where he had counted to, so he gave that up.

They came to a widening in the tunnel, a cavern with stalagmites and stalactites, some of them joining to form natural pillars of limestone. The place had the feel about it of a church: silent, set apart, holy. And then he saw the paintings. All the smooth parts of the walls were filled with paintings of animals, black and red and yellow. Alec had learned about cave paintings in school and knew the pigments were made from soot, and from red and yellow ochre, mixed with animal grease. He also knew that they were ancient, but these looked fresh, as if they had been done yesterday. Here was a stag with a great rack of antlers, and here a horse – no thoroughbred, but a short-legged stocky pony with a long tangle of mane and tail. Over there, in the corner, a boar, tusked and bristling. The artist, whoever he was, had captured the beasts in movement, carefully observed from life.

Alec had the sudden, dizzying feeling that he was travelling back in time, first to old-fashioned Mrs. Tickle, then to the very primitive farmer and his small cows, and now to the earliest beginnings of human culture, thousands of years ago. What next? He wondered. Dinosaurs perhaps? He hoped not. At last, he tore himself away from the wonderful cave and followed Mog through the entrance to another tunnel, until a pale light began to suffuse the gloom and they emerged into daylight. But they were at a high elevation, on the top of a cliff. Alec looked out across a black landscape that was bare except for a clearly defined roadway which appeared to spring from the base of the cliff. That suggested use by others, and he found that comforting. The tunnel had not climbed; at least it had not seemed to, but the land on this side of the massive outcrop of limestone was lower than that on the other. Of course, he was going west, towards the sea. The land would slope towards it. He looked for steps in the rock. Surely whoever had gouged out the tunnel would have built a staircase, a means to get down. But there was none.

"How are we to get down, Mog? Have we come so far to be forced to go back?"

And then Mog did a terrifying thing. As Alec stood on the edge of the cliff, Mog suddenly jumped up at him and pushed him. With a great cry Alec fell forward into space. But he didn't fall. He floated slowly, gently to the ground. After the first spine-chilling panic he found the sensation delightful. He felt as if the air was as dense as water and he was swimming in it. As his feet touched the ground, Mog landing gently beside him, he turned and looked back at the glowering face of the cliff, hardly able to believe what had just happened

"The rules are different here, aren't they, Mog?" he whispered. "I feel as if I am being protected and guided not only but you. Truly I need fear no evil."

Chapter 7
Apprenticeship

Sarah set a bowl of porridge in front of Roger. There was an earthenware pitcher of milk on the kitchen table, and a bowl of brown sugar. Roger was hungry again and fell to with a will. Sarah sat down opposite him, her strong hands around a mug of tea. She smiled at him.

"Our son was going to be the apprentice," she said. "Then in time he would have inherited the business."

"Would have?"

"Randall went for a soldier in the war. He never came back."

"I… I'm sorry." Roger had no idea what to say. What can one say to such a thing? Sarah's expression was infinitely sad.

"Simon never talks about him," she said. "Different people deal with grief in different ways. He shuts it up inside him. I find that talking about him eases the pain."

A young woman came quietly into kitchen.

"We have our daughter," said Sarah, smiling and reaching out her hand to the girl.

Roger jumped clumsily to his feet.

"This is Janet," said Sarah. "Janet, this is Roger. He's going to be your father's apprentice. Isn't that nice?"

Janet looked hard at him and then turned away.

"Is it?" she said.

Sarah laughed.

"You'll need to be nice to him, Janet," she said. "He'll be living with us, so you'll see him every day."

Janet shrugged. She poured a cup of tea for herself and sat down beside her mother. She was plainly dressed and her hair was a brown braid that hung down her back. Her hands were those of someone who works with them. She turned her sky-blue eyes on Roger and studied his face intently, almost as though she meant to draw it.

"Where do you come from, young man?" she asked.

"From a small town to the north of here, about two days journey."

"What are you running away from?"

"Janet!" scolded her mother.

Roger laughed at this unexpected question.

"I didn't run from anything," he said. "More like running to something. There is no work to be had up there, so I set off to look for it. Yesterday your parents found me. I can't believe my luck – and their great kindness."

"Oh well, I suppose that's all right then," Janet conceded and sipped her tea thoughtfully.

Just then another girl crept into the kitchen, a thin, pale, timid little thing in a plain dress and a white apron that was too big for her tiny frame.

"And this is Nelly," said Sarah. "She helps us with the housework. Help yourself to tea, Nelly, and come and sit with us."

"Nelly makes up the fires in the morning, sweeps the house, does all the laundry," said Sarah. "I don't know what we'd do without her."

Nelly blushed and hung her head.

"Nelly is an orphan," Janet said, "a foundling in fact. No one knows where she came from or who her parents were."

Nelly blushed a deeper red, and Sarah said quickly, "We're very glad she came to live with us. Why, if Nelly wasn't here, dear Janet would have to do the laundry and make the fires."

"Oh, Ma!" It was Janet's turn to blush. Roger noticed a sly little smile on Nelly's face. He thought, "These two girls don't like each other very much. I hope I won't have to spend much time with them."

"Well, time to get on," announced Sarah as she stood up. "Janet, you and I have a deal of yarn to spin this day. Nelly, finish clearing away and then come and join us." She smiled at Nelly, who scowled back at her. "Roger, you'll find Simon waiting for you in the loft."

Roger climbed the stairs to the top of the house and entered the cavernous loft that occupied the whole top floor. The north wall was made entirely of window panes, and there were skylights in the steeply gabled roof. The room was filled with light on this fine morning. At one end of the loft was an enormous loom. Two others, smaller but still quite big, stood in the middle of the room. Nearest to the door was a small loom standing on a table. The south wall had a long table and a row of cupboards. Tiers of shelves covered the last wall, on which were bolts of cloth of many colors and weaves. Baskets held skeins of yarn, soberly colored for the most part.

"What work do Mrs. Webster and Janet do?" asked Roger.

"Why, they are the spinsters," said Simon "They spin the yarn we use in our weaving."

"But Mrs. Webster is not a spinster."

"She was when she began," said Simon. "That's how we met. She was learning the craft from my master's wife. I saw her sitting in a patch of sunlight, twirling her distaff, looking so intent and so demure – and so very pretty," he smiled, "and I was done for. The women spin and the men weave," he went on. "All very traditional."

"You may start with the table loom, Roger. It's a good way to begin. Let me show you. I have already started a small piece of cloth, just as a test piece, you understand. You can carry on with it and tomorrow I'll show you how to set up, but first I want you to get the feel and the rhythm of it. These up-and-down threads are the warp. When you press this lever, some of the wrap threads move upwards and leave a space. You throw the shuttle through the space, like this, and catch it with your other hand. Then you pull this bar forward _ it's called a beater – to push the weft thread tight against the others. Then you press this other lever, and – see that? – the upper thread moves back down and those bottom ones move up. Then you throw the shuttle back, like so, use the beater to push this weft thread into place and you have two rows of weft thread against the others you've already done. You'll find as you get used to it that will ease into a rhythm. Have you got all of that?"

"Yes, I think so," said Roger.

"Well, sit down on the bench and make the start. It doesn't matter if you make mistakes; this is just a test piece. I'll be over here on a big loom. As you can see, it has foot pedals to move the warp instead of your levers. Don't hesitate to ask questions."

Roger found the small loom quite easy to work. After a little, Simon came to check.

"Getting the hang of it?"

"Yes, thank you, sir."

They worked in companionable silence until noon, the two looms making rhythmic clacking sounds which Roger found soothing. Then Simon stood up and led the way downstairs for the mid-day meal. The women joined them for their simple repast.

"No ale at noon on workdays," said Simon. "Will you have milk or water?"

Roger found that his mouth was dry from the dust of the weaving loft and gratefully quaffed a tall mug of water in a single draught. As they prepared to go back upstairs, Sarah said, "Let me show you the other half of the cloth-making process."

The two men followed her into a sunny room at the back of the house. Sarah's low stool stood beside a spinning wheel. Janet had set down her distaff on another, taller stool. On the long wall of the room stood a bench beside a black iron stove, and on the stove sat two huge black cauldrons, steaming gently. On the bench were piles of yarn of various thickness, some pale grey in color, others a pale oatmeal shade. At right angles on another wall stretched several lines of rope, and from these hung long trails of yarn in many colors. Bushel baskets of raw wool stood beside a third stool.

"This is where we prepare the yarn," said Sarah. "Nelly cards the wool, and washes it, and dyes it. Then she hangs it up and dry, as you see. We wind it into skeins and Nelly carries the finished yarn up to the loft."

"I noticed her hands were stained," remarked Roger.

"That's from the dye. But her hands are also very soft. Show him your hands, Nelly. That's from the natural oil in the wool."

Sulkily, Nelly reached out her open hands and Roger could see they were indeed as soft as silk.

"What kind of dye do you use?" he asked.

"Different dyes, mostly natural vegetable dyes," said Sarah. "Lichens make fine dyes in warm, earthy shades. That big pot contains a type of lichen called old man's beard. It hangs from tree branches in the wood at the edge of town. It's green when we gather it, but it makes a pale orangish dye. Onion skins a fine brown dye. The stronger you make the solution and the longer you cook it, the darker the shade, of course. Then we use a mordant such as alum to make the color fast. The lichens don't need a mordant. We used to use woad for blue and indeed it gives a fine color. But the smell is terrible. So bad that woad dyers live apart on the edge of town and marry within their own community. Now we prefer to use indigo, but that comes from the Indies, as you can guess from the name. It's more costly, but it doesn't stink out the whole house, and we can use the same vat over and over as the dye shades from dark blue to light."

Simon laughed. "A great benefit," he said, "and well worth the money."

Roger noticed that Sarah did all the talking and spoke of Nelly almost as though she was not there. But surely her work was skilled also. He made a point of saying, "Thank you, Nelly, that's very interesting. I can see I have a lot to learn."

She gave him a brief, shy smile before scurrying back to her stool in the corner.

Sarah took her place at the wheel and began to spin it by pressing her foot lightly on the pedal. Janet picked up her distaff and sat on her stool. She twirled the distaff skillfully between her fingers and drew out the thread carefully with her other hand.

"Time to leave the ladies for now," said Simon jovially. "Back to the loft for us."

And so, the work continued for day after day, peacefully, rhythmically, harmoniously. Roger settled in comfortably and learned quickly because he found the weaving interesting. He soon progressed from the table loom to one of the foot looms. He and Simon worked side by side, usually in silence. Evening meals were the time for conversation, about spinning and weaving, for the most part, but sometimes with a spice of local gossip. Roger noticed that although Nelly took her meal with them, she sat mutely at the end of the table. She was treated more like a servant than a member of the family and it was clear that she resented it. He went out of his way to say good morning to her, and thank you.

Thus began Roger's apprenticeship to the weavers' trade.

Chapter 8
Trial by Fire

Alec tramped all day, keeping a steady pace, feeling no weariness. As the sun sank towards the horizon it shone directly into his eyes and dazzled him. He could hardly see where he was going, so he stopped a while and sat on the warm grass until the sun sank at last below the horizon, and purple twilight washed over the landscape.

It must be very late, thought Alec, "But I don't understand why the sun has set at last when it seemed to stand still for so long. Still, I may as well keep on as long as there is enough light to see by."

The purple sky darkened slowly to indigo, and a few stars shone out. As last it grew very dark and the black sky was filled with a shimmer of stars so thick that he could hardly make out the familiar constellations. They provided enough light to show him his way, until he came to a wall of rock that blocked his path. Over it and around it was a grassy mound and on the face of the stone he saw patterns carved: spirals and circles and wave forms. And then he heard the music: high voices raise in a song that was unlike any he had ever heard.

How beautiful they are, the lordly ones,
Who dwell in the hills, in the hollow hills…?

It seemed to be coming from the other side of the wall, and then he saw that a thin streak of light shone out of the wall, a straight line from top to bottom. He put his eye to the crack and was amazed by what he saw. It was a great cavern, illuminated by many torches and crowded with people. They were beautiful to look at, golden in the torchlight, dressed in flowing garments of green and white, with flowers in their hair. One caught sight of Alec and pointed him out to his neighbors. Then slowly, the crack in the stone opened until it was wide enough for Alec to squeeze through.

"Come in, traveler," they called in their musical voices. "Come in and feast with us. For this is the shortest night of the year and must not be wasted."

One reveler thrust a cup into Alec's hand. The drink was sweet, tasting of honey and wild flowers. He drank deeply and at once began to feel slightly dizzy. A girl seized his hand and, laughing, drew him into the center of the dance. The music grew faster and wilder, as they danced and laughed in each other's arms. Alec felt as if his head might fly away and his legs fall off, and still she made him dance.

"Do you like this?" she asked him, "Do you like me?"

"I think you are very beautiful," Alex replied. "And very dangerous."

That made her laugh again, her musical tinkling laughter like the sound of a stream flowing over rocks. At last she released him and he sank gratefully onto a moss-covered bench. It was then that he noticed the boy. He must have been perhaps five years old. He was sturdily built and his round face was covered with freckles. Of all that merry company he alone looked sad.

"Who are you?" Alec asked him.

"I'm Tom," said the boy. "I just woke up here one morning. Went to sleep in my own bed and woke up here. I want to go home."

Just then, Alec's dancing partner whirled past them and stopped suddenly when she saw them talking to each other.

"Why, Tom," she said, "we have found a friend for you. Now you will be happy."

"I'm not happy," replied Tom sulkily, "I want to go home."

"You always say that," said the girl "but soon you will grow used to your new life and forget your old one."

"What? Forget my mum and my dad and Rover and Dobbin and my little room under the eaves? Never! Never!"

"You stole him," cried Alec.

"We took him so he could be happy here. He will never be sick or hungry, never grow up or old. Why can't you be happy, you ungrateful child?"

Alec drew her a little way off and asked her "What of his parents? They will be grieving for him."

The girl wrinkled her brow.

"Grieving?" she echoed. "Why would they do that? They will have forgotten all about him when they have other children."

"You don't understand, do you?" said Alec angrily, "about love. About the love of parents for their children." She shrugged her shoulders.

"Love, grief," she said, "nothing lasts forever in your world."

"In my world? In our world? What do you mean?"

But Alec thought he might be beginning to understand and he grew afraid. He must escape from here, he thought, and take the boy with him if he could.

The girl seemed to read his thoughts.

"He can never go back," she said, "His parents are long dead and the world is changed. It doesn't matter for you. You can leave now if you will, for your journey is not yet finished, but Tom must stay here with us." She turned to the company.

"Our guest wishes to leave us," she announced.

"So soon? Why such haste? Does he not like us?" One said, "We will not let you go."

The girl said, "I have already given him leave."

"At least let him come with us to greet the sun on this the longest day of the year," said another.

Alec was puzzled. "Sometimes you talk as if no time was passing here and sometimes you observe time. How can you do both?"

"We choose," she said simply.

"But this isn't the summer solstice. It's late summer. I was picking ripe berries when I set out on my journey. The earth takes three hundred and sixty-five days to circle around the sun. We don't choose."

"That is your reality," said the fairy, "we choose our own reality. It is not entangled with yours."

The troop of the fair folk paraded out of the door of the mound, surrounding Alec and drawing him with them. They were singing again in their high thin voices as some played drums and whistles. The music sounded like wind in the trees, waves on the shore, running water The stolen child they left behind in the mound with a few to guard him. They danced up to the summit of the nearby green hill where a great pyramid of tree branches stood outlined against the slowly lightening sky. One carried a small leather pouch and out of it he took a flat piece of oak wood, a large dry fungus, a wisp of old man's beard and a wimble – a short wooden spindle pointed at one end. The singing stopped as the company gathered around him. He knelt to his task, placing the mushroom and the wisps of lichen near his hand. He set the pointed end of the wimble in a hollow in the oak and began to twist it between his palms, first one way then the other as his companions watched silently. A wisp of smoke rose. He touched the lichen to it and it too began to smoke, then to glow and suddenly a tiny flame flickered and grew. The company murmured softly as the firelighter fed more lichen to the flame and then the mushroom punk, slowly and carefully. He stood up and carried the glowing bundle to the bonfire. He touched it to the thin dry twigs at the bottom of the heap and at once they caught the flame and fed it.

Everyone applauded. Laughing and exclaiming, they joined hands and circled the growing fire and began to sing again, dancing sunwise, hand in hand. They drew Alec into the circle. The girl he had danced with held one hand and the fire maker held the other. The circle spun faster and faster until Alec felt breathless and giddy but he could not free his hands as the landscape whirled around him. He saw the sun slowly rising and at the precise moment when it cleared the horizon he felt a hard push between his shoulder blades. He fell forward directly into the fire. He screamed, flailing his arms wildly in panic. He braced himself for the pain but he felt none. The fire was all around him but he was not harmed by it. For a long moment, he saw the others through the red and flickering flames and they were laughing, but then he was pulled back by those who gripped his hands. Alec was dragged sobbing and stumbling, coughing and blinded by tears but not burned. The wild dance did not pause as the flames rose higher and consumed the bonfire. The company at last let go of each other's hands and sank to the ground breathless and laughing.

"It is done," said the fire maker, "The fire is fed, the sun is strong, the harvest grows by seed and bud, by leaf and blossom. It is done."

The others echoed "It is done."

The girl turned to Alec. "You are free to go now," she said, "Westward lies your way. There are many paths but only one destination."

Chapter 9
Bonfire Night

The days were growing short, and it was dark now by supper time. The trees were shedding their gaudy autumn leaves and children were enjoying shuffling through the piles of dry leaves on the street. They went into the woods to collect conkers from the horse chestnut trees. Inside their spiky green casing the horse chestnuts were hard and brown and shiny. Small boys pierced a hole and threaded string through them. They took turns to hold up their conker by the string while another boy hit it with his. The aim was to smash the opponent's conker. Sometimes, the boys soaked them in vinegar to harden them. Sometimes one conker survived every skirmish and earned high prestige for the boy who owned it. Roger fondly remembered playing at conkers with Alec and his other friends.

He was looking forward to Bonfire Night, when Guy Fawkes was burned in effigy. Fawkes had plotted to kill the king, but he was caught just in time. The king's loyal subjects had lit bonfires in the streets to celebrate, and it had become an annual event here in England, where they did not observe the old tradition of Hallowe'en. Roger was interested to see how it would differ.

Whenever he went out, he was accosted by grubby children who thrust out their hands and called, "Penny for the guy, mister." They were the same children who had played at conkers. Now they were busy collecting firewood for their bonfires, not all of it dead and down branches from the woods. Roger noticed one or two fenceposts on the heap outside their house. In a wheelbarrow they had an effigy of Guy Fawkes, made from old clothes stuffed with straw. The pennies, Simon told him, were to buy fireworks.

"It will be your job to make sure the animals are all safely stalled and the stable doors locked," he told Roger. "Make sure we have buckets of water in case of sparks. Brooms and old horse blankets, too. Collect them and stack them by the barn. If it is rainy, we should be safe enough, but if the October winds still blow in November there will be surely be mishaps. And someone always gets hurt. Last year, a child lost an eye when he held on to a firecracker just a little too long. So, think on. I am relying on you."

"Yes, sir," said Roger. "I'll be careful. But sir, did you join in this when you were young?"

"Oh yes," nodded Simon, "and so did my son." His eyes misted a little. "When we are young, we are heedless of danger. We expect to live forever."

Then he clapped his hands together briskly, and the moment was gone.

"Let us get on," he said, "it will soon be dark and they will light the fire."

Men brought a ladder to lean against the pyramid of wood. One of them climbed the ladder and reached down as two others lifted up the guy. When it was secured among the topmost branches, he climbed down and the ladder was removed. It was the mayor who had the honor of lightning the fire, touching an old-fashioned torch to the bottom of the pile. The flames began to lick at the twigs, and then to grow. Soon, flames leapt up with a roar and a crackle, and the bonfire was well and truly lit. Everyone cheered.

"A very, very long time ago," said Sarah, "they used to burn a real man, as a sacrifice to their heathen gods. Then they began making the straw man instead, and at last he was identified with the traitor, Guy Fawkes. We keep the custom because it is a festival which everyone can enjoy, lightning as the year darkens."

By this time the flames had reached the guy, which began first to smolder and then to burn fiercely as the straw ignited. Fireworks tucked inside it exploded and sent showers of scarlet sparks rising upwards before they fell again like bright rain. Roger noted where they fell, and stamped on a few, but there was no danger to roofs. He joined hands with the people on either side of him as they circled the fire, loudly chanting:

Remember, remember, the fifth of November, Gunpowder treason and plot.
I see no reason why gunpowder treason should ever… be…forgot!

Roger realized that the hands he was holding were Janet's and Nelly's and felt suddenly shy, but the girls seemed to regard it as an acceptable element of the celebration, so he did too. It seemed to him after a while that Janet was holding his hand very tightly. He squeezed her hand gently and she responded with pressure in return. He looked at her and she was smiling at him, her face rosy in the firelight, her eyes sparkling. People lit fireworks and filled the sky with colored stars and comets, red and blue and green. The children exclaimed in wonder and delight.

"I should stand by with the water and the blankets," said Roger.

"Let me help you," said Janet, and then, "Nelly, we don't need your help. Stay and enjoy the fireworks."

Janet followed Roger, still grasping his hand. They stood together in front of the barn where the buckets and brooms were piled, watching carefully, but this year all was well. Although the sky was clear, there was not a breath of wind. The grownups kept their watchful eyes on the older boys, and no one was hurt this year. As the fire began to die down, people drifted away. Parents carried sleepy children home to bed, and couples wandered off into the darkness. The men who had built the bonfire had the duty of staying until it was safely burnt out.

Janet turned, smiling, to Roger.

"Was this your first bonfire night?"

"Yes. We don't do this in Scotland."

"You should. It was the Scottish king they were plotting against. Did you enjoy the evening?"

"Very much. yes."

"It's still not very late," said Janet. "We could walk as far as the riverbank."

Roger's heart began to beat faster. She led him down the barn to the river, and they stood together on the smooth grass of the bank.

"A full moon tonight," she said, "with a ring around it. It will rain tomorrow and that will make sure there are no embers still smoldering."

"I hardly noticed the moon among all the other lights," said Roger.

"It rose only an hour ago," said Janet, "it has only just cleared the rooftops. Now it's shining down just for us."

Roger's heart beat faster than ever.

Suddenly, not looking at him, Janet said, "Would you like to make love to me?"

Roger gasped, "What?"

"Well, would you?"

"Yes, very much, but we can't, can we?"

Janet laughed. "Why not?"

"Because we're not married. I owe everything to your parents and would never betray the trust they have shown in me."

"Then you will have to marry me!" cried Janet, triumphantly.

"Is that what you want?"

Janet's tone become suddenly practical and business-like.

"It often happens that an apprentice marries his master's daughter. My brother is dead, so I shall inherit the business. It would be the sensible thing to do."

"Not very romantic," said Roger.

Janet smiled. "Making love is romantic. Marriage is for living."

"Then yes," said Roger. "Let us be married. I'll ask your father tomorrow."

"That's settled then," said Janet comfortably. "You may kiss me if you like."

So, Roger did.

Chapter 10
Trial by Water

Alec was glad to escape from these strange people . They were beautiful and glamorous, but they frightened him. There was something about them, he would have been hard pressed to name it – some lack of feeling, of sympathy. They seemed not to understand the homesickness of the child, Tom, or the grief his loss might cause his parents. The trick of shoving him into the fire and pulling him out again was terrifying. He did not understand why he was not hurt, but he shuddered when he thought how he might have been. He was sure it had not been an accident. So he hastened away from that place, Mog trotting patiently by his side, his presence comforting in this empty landscape.

At last, he came to a place where the road dipped towards a broad stream that flowed sluggishly in the flat land. The road spanned it by means of a sturdy wooden bridge. Alec paused at the crown of the bridge and looked down into the water. It was so clear that he could see the sand at the bottom, the gently swaying weeds and the small silver fishes that darted among them. His own face stared up at him and then with a start of surprise he saw the reflection of another face, grinning over his shoulder. He turned quickly to find himself looking into the sparkling green eyes of a pretty girl. Everything about her was green; not only her dress but also her long hair which cascaded about her shoulders like the weeds in the water. Even her skin had a slightly green tinge.

"You startled me," he exclaimed.

"You had your back to me," she said, "I wanted to see your face."

"Well, now that you have seen it, how do you like it?"

"It's a good face," she said, giving him a long and careful scrutiny. "Not handsome, but honest and, yes, humorous. How are you called?"

"I'm Alec," he told her. "What's your name?"

"I am Avon," she said.

"Avon," he repeated. "That's an unusual name."

"It's an old word which means river," she answered. "This is my river. I am of the river."

"Do you mean you are some kind water nymph?" Alec started to laugh, and then he realized that she was quite serious, *she must be mad, poor thing,* he thought. "I must be gentle with her, but careful too. She might have pushed me in when she crept up behind me like that. Perhaps she meant to. Still, it's clean and not deep."

He glanced at Mog; the dog was sitting quietly watching them both. He showed no sign of alarm or hostility. By this time Alec had learned to trust the dog's responses, and had ceased to wonder why he had made himself scarce during the robbery.

Avon smiled. "Would you like to make love to me?" she asked.

Alec gasped. "What? We have only just met and – well – ah!"

71

"Would you like to?" she persisted.

"Well, yes, of course. You are lovely. But it would be wrong – wouldn't it?"

"Why?"

"Well, ah, we're not married."

Avon laughed. "What does marriage have to do with it?" she asked. "We can make love here, in the water, and then you will go and I shall stay. We shall make each other happy for a little while, until the memory fades."

"Do you always ask this of wayfarers?"

"Always, but there are so few nowadays," she added sadly. "Let us seize the moment. Come, step into the river with me. I'll make you glad you did."

Mog stretched himself upon the ground and shut his eyes. Alec took a deep breath and stepped into the stream. The water had been warmed by the sun. As it rippled and flowed around him, he could not tell which gentle caress was that of the water or that of her fingers. She tugged at his knees until he lost his balance and fell submerged in the clear water. He struggled up, and Avon pulled him down again.

She means to drown me, he thought, *I escape the fire and now the water will get me.*

He began to flail in panic. But then he found himself floating on his back with Avon beside him, caressing him and kissing him with slow gentleness.

"I forgot you couldn't breathe in my element," she whispered, "No matter, do you not yet understand? You no longer need to breathe."

He stared at her.

"This will be the last time for you," she told him, "Do not waste it. Then you must complete your journey."

And so they lay together in the water all the long, languid summer afternoon, as the sun sank slowly down the western sky and the moon rose, full and silver in the east. The water began to grow chill.

"Go now," Avon whispered.

Alec climbed out of the stream and found he was perfectly dry and fully clothed. He turned to look back at her and she was nowhere to be seen. Only the rippling water and the green waving weeds. Mog jumped his feet and gave one short bark, as if to say "let us go." So, Alec followed him towards the crimson sunset. He looked back once or twice but saw no trace of Avon. And still, he felt neither tired nor hungry.

"I no longer need to breathe," he repeated. "Do I not yet understand?"

Suddenly he was filled with fear.

"How can I be dead?" he wondered. "I cannot remember dying. Was it the wild men in the forest? Have I been dead all this time? Is that why I feel no hunger? Is what why the fire did not burn me? Is that the journey I must make? And what shall I find at journey's end?"

He gazed down into Mog's amber yes.

"I think you knew, didn't you? I think you are the Moggy Dhu, the black dog who guide the souls of the dead."

Mog nodded his head.

"But it's all different," Alec cried. "The Moggy Dhu is just a superstition of the unlettered country folk. This is not what I was taught when I was growing up! Oh, Lord," he thought. "Is my journey leading me to heaven – or to hell? I have spent the day in sin, with a water nymph, another old superstition. Oh Lord, have mercy on me." He fell to his knees and wept.

Chapter 11
Family Matters

The next day Roger sought an opportunity to speak to Simon and Sarah. He felt very nervous and tried not to show it. He clasped his hands behind his back so they couldn't see them shaking. He cleared his throat.

"I have something to ask you," he began.

"Yes, my boy?"

"It would be a great favor and a great honor…"

"Go on."

"I wonder if you could see your way… to consider … to… please, I want to marry Janet."

There was a hint of laughter in his voice as Simon asked, "And does she want to marry you?"

"Yes sir, at least, she told me so."

Sarah and Simon smiled at each other, the kind of smile that conveys much information, the kind of smile exchanged and understood by people who have known and loved each other for a lifetime.

Then Simon said, "We are not surprised by this. We have been expecting it, in fact."

"You have?"

"Oh yes," nodded Sarah. "We have noticed the signs."

Roger felt himself blushing.

"But I never spoke to her before yesterday," he said, "How could you possibly tell?"

"My dear boy," said Simon, "we have been where you are now. Well do I remember asking Sarah's father for her hand. And how nervous I was."

"Young people forget," added Sarah, "that old people were young once too. And we do not forget."

"Well, young man," said Simon, suddenly very businesslike. "I am pleased with your progress in your apprenticeship. In a few months you will advance to the status of journeyman and in a year or two, if all goes well, you will qualify as a master weaver and a full Guild member. On that day you may marry our daughter. Until then, you may announce your betrothal."

"Oh, thank you, thank you, sir."

"But – betrothal is not marriage. Your friendship must remain chaste. Who knows what may happens in two years?"

Sarah looked at Roger tearfully.

"Our son should have inherited the business. Now it will go to our son-in-law. I hope you will be he."

Roger's eyes filled with tears also.

"Everything I have and everything I hoped for I owe to you," he said. "I will not betray your trust in me; it is too precious to lose."

Sarah rose, saying, "I must find Janet; I'll bring her here."

Simon said, "I have been observing you, Roger, not only for your progress in the trade but also for you character. I bless the day we found you on the road and brought you home. Now, I believe you said you have a widowed mother?"

"Yes, sir."

"You must write to her at once to tell her your happy news. Sarah will add a note inviting her to come and stay with us if she so wishes. Would it be insulting to enclose the cost of the coach fare?"

"You think of everything, sir," Roger answered. "But I have been sending her a portion of my wages. I think she is used to thrift and will have put some of it away."

Sarah came back into the parlor, leading a blushing Janet by the hand.

"My darling girl," said Simon, "I think you have made a wise choice. Your mother and I are delighted. I think this young fellow is quite pleased too."

Then he burst into tears.

"Ring for tea, Janet," said her mother.

When Nelly arrived with the tray, she was amazed to find all of them laughing and weeping together.

"Nelly, dear," burst out Sarah. "We have wonderful news. Roger and Janet are engaged to be married."

Nelly let out a loud wail and fled from the room.

"What was that about?" asked Simon, bewildered.

"Papa, Nelly is in love with Roger too," said Janet.

Roger blushed again.

"I had no idea," he said. "I certainly did nothing to make her think I was interested in her. Alas, I would not have hurt her for the world, poor Nelly."

"Poor Nelly indeed," agreed Janet, ever practical. "At least she had time to set down the tea tray."

"Go and comfort her, my dear," said Simon.

"In a little while," said Sarah. "Let her weep in private first."

And so their joyful tea party was sobered by this discordant note. They had all taken Nelly for granted, they realized and treated her more like a piece of furniture than a person with feelings.

"We must give some thought to Nelly and what is best for her," said Sarah.

She busied herself with pouring the tea, and when they were all served, Roger drew out a sheet of paper from his pocket.

"I received a letter from Ma just other day," said Roger. This is what she wrote:

"My dear Son, I am rite glad to have good news. I never doubted you would do well, but your grate good luck is something we could not have counted on. The Lord has blessed you and I trust you will thank him. There is no news here, still no work, I miss you and hope your master will let you come and visit. Your loving Mother."

"But of course, you must go home for a visit!" exclaimed Sarah. "Go as soon as it's convenient, and bring her back with you, if she is willing."

So, Roger took the wagon and drove the north, noting, as he passed the place on the road where he had met Simon and Sarah, the apothecary's shop and the inn where he fallen prey to the press gang.

I wish I could find the man who rescued me, he thought, but I wouldn't know how to begin looking for him. He never told me his name, and I never thought to ask.

When at last he reached his home town, he found it just as grey and cheerless as he remembered, and also somehow smaller. He halted the wagon outside his mother's cottage and tethered Daisy to the gatepost. His heart began to beat a little faster as he approached the door and tapped on it. He heard from the depths of the house his mother's beloved voice calling, "Coming!" The door opened and there she was, quite unchanged, just as though he had left her not an hour ago. Her eyes and mouth opened wide and her cheeks turned pale. She pressed her hand to her heart. Then she smiled, the color rushing back into her face, her eyes brimming with tears.

"Roger, my dear, my darling boy!" she cried. "Come in, come in do, I'm so happy to see you."

As he stepped inside the familiar cozy room, she hugged him and he hugged her back, feeling very near to tears himself.

"I'll put the kettle on," she said.

Watching her going through the familiar ritual of making the tea, Roger told her about his engagement, and about his progress in his apprenticeship. Cathy raised her hands to her mouth, laughing and crying together. Then she hugged him again, but her heart was too full for words.

"Mr. and Mrs. Webster want to invite you to come and live with them – with us. I'd like that very much. is there anything to keep you here?"

"Not really," said Cathy, "I have neighbors who are friendly but no close friends. I don't own this cottage, I just rent it, as you know. If you hadn't been sending money I would have had to go on the parish. You are all I care for in the world, being near you is all I want, or need."

"Then you'll come? You'll come back with me now?"

"Yes, Roger," she said "Tomorrow, if you like. I'll have to tell the landlord, but the rent's paid up to the end of the month. And the furniture goes with the cottage. Let's go to the Thistle for our supper. You can sleep there, or here on the couch, and tomorrow we'll pack my things on your wagon and go, early."

Over supper at the Thistle, Roger told his mother more about the Websters, and about spinning and weaving. Cathy said very little, listening intently, her eyes shining with pride. It was still early when they walked home and went to bed, Roger on the sofa, and they were up with the first light in the morning. As Roger loaded the wagon with her few things, Cathy hurried to the landlord's house. He was not very pleased to be wakened so early or to be given such short notice about the cottage, but he grudgingly wished her well. As she closed the door, he was already calculating that if he could find another tenant at once, he would receive two lots of rent for the half month remaining. *There's always a silver lining,* he thought.

Roger fed Daisy her oats, and helped his mother up to the seat of the wagon. They stopped at the water trough so that Daisy could drink, and then they were off.

"My goodness," said Cathy, a little breathless. "This has all happened so fast. What an adventure!"

They came to the Cat and Pigeons. Roger flicked the reins and urged Daisy to a brisk trot until they were safely past.

"What's the matter?" asked Cathy. "Why are you hurrying? We might stay at that inn for the night."

"Did that on my first journey," said Roger tersely. "Not a nice place. Not suitable for a lady. But there is one place I must stop."

He drew up before the apothecary's shop and tethered Daisy to the hitching post by the door.

"I'll be just a minute, Ma," he said. "No need for you to climb down."

He could see a light in the back of the shop. He opened the door and walked in. The apothecary was absorbed in the task of grinding something with a mortar and pestle, but he looked up as the bell above the door jangled.

"You!" he said.

"Yes, me," grinned Roger. "I wanted you to know that I fared well after I left you. I recovered quickly from my injuries, and I have an apprenticeship. I can now afford to pay you what I owe for your care."

"My dear boy, you owe me nothing. Not a penny." He looked through the window at Cathy perched on the wagon. "Who is the lady?"

"She is my mother. I never told her about the press gang. I don't want her to know. Look, let me give you a sovereign, to pay for the next poor soul who can't afford to pay you."

"There is no need."

"I need," said Roger. "I need to share my luck. It's important. Do you understand?"

"Ah, yes," agreed the apothecary. "I understand very well. Good luck is a kind of debt. I will take your sovereign and do as you ask. God bless you, boy."

"Who was that?" asked Cathy when he climbed back on to the wagon.

"Just a man. I stopped here on my first journey and he gave me tea. I just wanted him to know about my good fortune. Now we must find a respectable hostelry to spend the night."

And so they did, arriving at the Websters' on the next afternoon. Sarah came running out of the door when she heard the horse's hoofs on the cobbles.

"My dear," she cried, smiling and holding out her hands to Cathy. "You are most welcome for Roger's sake, and for your own sake too, of course. Did you have a good journey? Come in and sit down. Nelly, we'd like tea, please."

All this is one breath.

Simon, more formal, shook her hand.

"We are very glad you agreed to come," he said. "Come and rest after your journey, while Roger sees to Daisy."

As they were having tea and becoming acquainted, Simon said, "Roger shows real aptitude for the weavers' trade and appears to enjoy it. We all like what we're good at, and we're good at what we like. Sarah and I had a son, Randall was his name. It was my plan to train him, and for him to inherit the business in the fullness of time. But he died. He died. Killed in the war."

"I am so very sorry," murmured Cathy.

"Your son has become like an own son to Sarah and me. I would like him to inherit the business, and I would like to adopt him formally and give him my name, with your permission. And his too, of course."

He smiled at Roger who sat open-mouthed, unable to speak.

"What do you say, Roger?"

"I…I…I would like that very much," he stammered. "An honor."

Sarah said, "And you, dear Cathy, will be family. I promise not to try to take your place in Roger's heart."

Cathy said, "If I am to live here as a member of your family, you must let me do my share."

"No, no," said Sarah, "that doesn't matter."

"It matters to me. Let me cook for you."

"She's a wonderful cook," said Roger proudly.

"Perhaps you'd like to join us spinsters?" suggested Sarah.

So, it was decided. Roger became Roger Webster. Cathy supervised the kitchen, being careful to treat Nelly with kindness, and worked in the afternoons in the spinning room, learning and chatting and becoming so much a part of the family that it was hard to remember a time when she was not.

Chapter 12
The Sisters

Alec and Mog continued on their way, following the trail across the endless plain. Gradually the landscape began to change. Tufts of grass, sparse at first, but slowly the tufts expanded into meadow, green and flower-spangled and fragrant under a sky of clear blue, still their shadows long before them, as if the sun had not moved and no time had passed. Alec hardly noticed any longer. He had given up trying to fit this strange place into the patterns he thought he knew. A blue haze ahead of them slowly resolved itself into a line of trees, the edge of a wood, but these trees had lost all their leaves – black branches against the pale sky. And yet at his feet the grass was green and the flowers, buttercups and daisies, dandelions and clover, tiny violets and the white star flower of wild strawberries, had the look of early summer.

As they were enjoying the warm sunshine and the scent of the grass and wild flowers, suddenly a large winged insect flew towards them, making a loud buzzing sound. It was not a bee, but some kind of ugly black fly, and it took no interest in the flowers. It tried to alight on Alec's face. He flailed at it, but it avoided his hands and returned to the attack. At once, it seemed, there was a swarm of the things, a very army, biting and stinging his head and neck and making him frantic.

"Where did they all come from so suddenly?" he wondered. "Could they smell me? It could seem no one has passed this way for a long time. They must be hungry. But they are not attacking Mog."

The dog trotted serenely beside him. There were no flies near him.

"You're lucky to have such a thick coat," Alec told him, "But I would have thought they might attack your nose and eyes. For goodness sake, get away from me, you wretched things!"

And suddenly they did. The swarm hovered in the air and stayed as he ran away from them. He was still looking behind him as he ran, when he tripped and fell headlong among the flowers. As he raised his head he saw before him a huge spider's web glistening with dewdrops like beads of crystal on a necklace. Beside it, poised motionless on a long blade of grass, sat a large black spider.

"Ugh!" exclaimed Alec, scrambling hastily to his feet.

Then as he looked about him he saw that the meadow all before him and around him was covered with spangled webs, each with its guardian spider. He shuddered. Then he realized that they were the reason the flies had halted, as though afraid to ventured into the spiders' domain. Indeed, a few of the webs held captured files, still feebly struggling.

I never thought I would be grateful to spiders, he thought, *or even pleased to see them.*

He laughed aloud.

"Thank you, Spiders," he called out. "Thank you, spinners and weavers and bane of flies."

Then it seemed to him that a narrow space appeared between the webs, forming a trail across the meadow towards the line of hills which rose gently about a mile or so away. In the middle of the meadow stood a tall ash tree, and seated on the ground at its roots were three women. They all wore grey clothes with grey shawls covering their grey hair. They seemed almost to be parts of the grey bark of the ash tree. Alec was struck by the contrast between this stark greyness and the green, flower-strewn meadow. One of them held a distaff on which she was spinning a length of thread. Another held a small handloom which rested on her knees. She took up the thread from the distaff and wove it into the fabric on her loom. The third woman sat motionless, in her lap a huge pair of silver scissors. They watched him intently as he approached. They seemed so out of place, sitting there far from any habitation. Mog growled softly, his ears flattened, his tail between his legs.

"Good day to you ladies," called Alec in as strong a voice as he could muster.

None of them acknowledged his greeting. They continued to sit silently and without moving as he drew nearer.

"Can you tell me, if you please, if this track leads to the seashore? I have been walking for many days (How many days? he wondered). I seem to have lost count – and I have somehow missed the road. I'm afraid I'm lost."

Then the first woman, the one with the distaff, said in a whispery voice:

"You are not lost."

The second woman, she with the loom on her knees added in a slightly stronger voice:

87

"You must continue on this trail. It will lead you to your destination."

The third women, whose voice was deep, said:

"All paths lead to the place where you are going. There are many paths but only one destination."

The way she said it made Alec shiver. There was a tone in her voice that sounded almost as though she were gloating.

"Well," he said, affecting cheerfulness he did not feel, "that is reassuring news. May I do anything to help you? You seem so far away from shelter or comfort."

The women shoot their heads simultaneously.

"This is our place," said the first.

"Under the ash tree," said the second.

"Always," said the third, "for even my sisters and I have a wyrd."

"Wyrd," Alec repeated. "That means fate, does it not?"

Suddenly, he gasped as he saw the connection. "You are the fates! Dear God, how have I come to this?"

The first sister nodded.

"At last," she said, "you have understood. I spin the thread which is a human life. This is your thread, your life."

"And I," said the second sister, "take the thread my sister spins, and I weave it into the tapestry, where it meets and intertwines with many other threads."

"And I," said the third sister, "cut each thread with my sharp shears. Your thread is very short, you see. My decisions are arbitrary and from them there is no appeal."

Alec gulped.

"Then I really am dead?" he whispered. "That is why I have lost track of time, and feel neither hunger nor thirst. Ah yes! The outlaws in the forest! And the dog?"

"He is your guide. His task is to take you into the west. Trust him."

"I do. I have. But I didn't realize…"

Alec sank down upon grass and put his head in his hands. Presently he looked up at them.

"Does everyone make this journey?" he asked.

"I told you," said the third sister. "There are many paths. You are young: there is much you have yet to learn, which most mortals have a lifetime to learn."

"And some never do," added the second sister.

"You may think yourself fortunate," said the first.

"Fortunate!" echoed Alec. "To have missed so much of life? So many joys?"

"And sorrows," said the weaver.

The thirst sister said, "Young people, cut off in their time, miss so much. All the learning and experience that go to make them human. So, they must have it here."

"It's all one, at the last," murmured the spinner. "Go now," said the third sister, "to the shore."

"And then?" asked Alec.

"That you will discover," she said. "Now go."

So, Alec stepped past them and continued walking, following Mog. After he had walked a few yards, he turned and looked back. The three sisters had disappeared. The tree remained but the women had vanished as though they had never been.

But from somewhere high in the heavens a voice rose in song – a woman's voice, a keening kind of song which sounded ancient and eerie. Alec recognized it, although he had never heard it before. It was the song of the banshee, the spirit that waits for the dead.

Chapter 13
Achievement

Roger served an apprenticeship of a year and a day. Then he was made a journeyman, a word that used to mean someone who is hired by the day. "Although I work by the year, not by the day," he joked. Now, three years later, for his masterpiece, he wove a length of fine woolen cloth in which he blended threads of sage green, periwinkle blue, and pale grey. All the thread was spun and dyed by Sarah and Janet and Cathy. The fabric seemed to shimmer as it caught the light. It was warm to wear but very light in weight. It folded and draped gracefully and never creased. This he presented proudly to the officers of the weaver's Guild, accompanied and sponsored by Simon, his master. The officers scrutinized the fabric with magnifying lenses, held it up to the light, scrunched it up and let it cascade softly without a wrinkle. They weighed it and draped it about their shoulders, all the while at pains to conceal their delight and pleasure in the wonderful stuff. Then they turned as one to Roger, smiling, and admitted him to the high degree of master weaver.

"Congratulations to you, too Master Webster," said the chairman, "you have taught him well."

"He has been a most apt and diligent pupil," answered Simon, beaming proudly.

There was a banquet of celebration that very evening. Roger was thrilled to be acknowledge by the masters as their peer. His speech recounted his fortunate meeting with Simon and Sarah, and once again professed his deep gratitude to them. In recognition of this, and with their permission, he declared his intention to take the name of Webster for his own.

Simon's speech informed the Guild that he would now make Roger a full partner in the firm, to be known henceforth as Webster and Son.

"He will be my son twice over," he said. "First by adoption and also by marriage. Mrs. Webster and I have given our blessing to the forthcoming marriage of Roger and our beloved only child, Janet."

The Masters cheered and applauded and there were many toasts: The old Master to the new Master, to the bride to be, and to the worshipful guild of weavers itself.

*****

Midsummer Day dawned warmed and golden. Roger and Simon hastened early to the church while the women were still dressing. For Simon reminded Roger that it is bad luck for bride and groom to see each other before the ceremony. Roger wore a coat made from his wonderful masterpiece material. He felt happy and excited and shy and apprehensive, all at the same time The Mayor had been invited, and the mayor's son had agreed to do the office of best man. "Second best man," he joked. All the local guild brethren were there, with their wives. They filled the little church, the men in formal dress, the women in their stiff gowns and pretty hats, trimmed with flowers and feathers. They chattered quietly to each other, ignoring the music of the organ.

Meanwhile at the Webster house, the women were very busy, teasing and laughing as they dressed. Janet's wedding gown was of white silk with lace over it, and she wore the veil of Belgian lace that Sarah had worn for her own wedding.

"Something old, something new," they chorused.

"Something borrowed," said Nelly, shyly offering her small white prayer book.

"And something blue," added Cathy triumphantly, as she fastened around Janet's neck a single star sapphire pendant on a silver chain. "I wore that at my wedding," she told Janet, "And my mother wore it at hers. It's yours now, dear Janet, my new daughter. May it bring you joy." Then they all had a gentle little weep, and dried their eyes on white lace handkerchiefs.

Nelly reported that Simon had returned to escort his daughter. They formed a small procession, Janet on Simon's arm, followed by Nelly in her pink muslin dress, carrying the bridal bouquet of pink roses, and the two mothers walked together arm in arm. There were many people gathered lining both sides of the street, clapping their hands and smiling, calling out best wishes for the bride. Janet was glowing with happiness. She looked radiantly beautiful as every bride does on her wedding day.

They came into the square and now they could hear the music of the organ. As they entered the church, the organist began the traditional wedding march. Simon led his daughter proudly down the aisle to the altar, where Roger and his best man were waiting along with the minister. Roger turned and his face lit up as he saw Janet, rosy and smiling at him through a froth of lace. He thought he had never been so happy. Simon gently took Janet's hand and laid it on Roger's arm.

"Dearly beloved," intoned the minister. He was speaking to the whole congregation, but for Janet and Roger it seemed the words were addressed only to them. The ceremony was dignified, but brief. As soon as they were formally pronounced man and wife, the newlywed couple walked back down the aisle together and out into the sunlit square while the bells pealed and the organ thundered. Standing on the steps of the church, Janet turned around and threw the bouquet over her shoulder. When she turned again, she was surprised to find that Nelly had not caught it. Another girl, a stranger, had leaped forward and stretched out her eager hands to snatch it. Now she held it aloft and crowed with delight as she brandished it like a trophy. Nelly had been quiet all day, but no one thought much of this. She was always quiet and withdrawn. But now she let out a sob and fled back into the dim and shadowy church. Sarah, concerned followed after her.

"Nelly my dear, whatever's the matter?" she asked.

"Go away," sobbed Nelly. "Leave me alone."

"But my dear…"

"I am not your dear, I never was. Don't pretend."

"I'm sorry you are so upset. I shall leave you be if that is your wish. When you are ready, come to the reception. The bridesmaid is expected to dance with the best man, you know. And who knows what may come of that?"

Nelly never came to the reception at the house, but everyone was so busy having fun that her absence was hardly noticed. The best man, very jolly and more than a little drunk, took his leave at last and with a final sally shouted up the stairs: "What sort of a bridegroom chooses the shortest night of the year?"

Then delighted by his own wit he reeled of the door.

"What a lovely day this has been," said Sarah to Simon when they were alone at last. "There was just one discordant note. Did you guess that Nelly was still in love with Roger?"

Chapter 14
Immortality

Alec fell to the ground and wept until he was exhausted, his face in his arms, his ribs heaving. After a while, Mog nudged him gently on the neck, and then again, a little more forcefully. Alec raised his swollen face. Mog whined softly and nudged him again.

"What is the point of going on?" wailed Alec. "I may as well stay here – in limbo, if that's where I am. Or purgatory, or just simply nowhere. Why don't you leave me?"

Mog whined again and tugged gently at Alec's sleeve.

"It's no use."

Then Mog sat back on his haunches and barked.

"Stop that," said Alec, "it won't make any difference."

Mog bared his teeth and growled softly, in the back of his throat.

"Yes, yes," said Alec irritably. "I can see you will not leave me be."

He struggled to his feet, squared his shoulders and took several deep, shuddering breaths.

"Lead me then," he said. "What more must I suffer in order to learn? And learn what? What I should have done? What I should not have done? It's too late for that. Here I am, a wretched sinner, on a journey to I know not where. But go on Mog, I will follow you."

On they trudged. Alec had no sense of time and indeed, the sun, perched on the western horizon and the moon in the east never moved. The sky above him was the deep purple of twilight and the green color had leached out of the landscape. There were no shadows. He accepted all of this numbly. He was beyond surprise or reason.

Presently they came to yet another area of forest, black against the last waning light of the western sky. There appeared to be a gap between the trees, like a natural gateway. Through it he could see the gloom of dense growth. As he followed Mog through the gap he felt a sudden cessation of sound and movement. The silence was complete… No furtive rustlings in the underbrush, no whisper of wind in leaves, not even his own footfalls. The wood felt lifeless. He was apprehensive, glancing about for signs of trouble. He picked up a stout stick that made him feel a little braver.

"Where are you taking me now, Mog? I am afraid of this place."

But Mog plodded on ahead of him and where he stepped a faint trail emerged.

"I'm glad you are with me, Mog," said Alec. "I don't think I would be brave enough to go on if you were not with me."

Mog gave him another of his long, knowing looks.

They emerged from the trees at last into a wide clearing, and in the middle of the clearing stood a great granite house, square and plain with no ornament, no color, no light in the blind windows. Alec made to go on the past the house but Mog walked purposefully up to a door made of wood so old it too had turned grey. The hinges and knocker were black iron.

"Am I supposed to knock?" Alec asked Mog. "Well, I no longer have any will or power to choose."

So, he lifted the great iron knocker and let it fall loudly, and heard the hollow echo within the house. He waited, but no one answered. Just as he was turning away the door swing open slowly but in complete silence.

This is the kind of door I would have expected to creak open, thought Alec, *now I suppose I must go in.*

So in he went, cautiously looking about him at a grey stone hallway with dark doors on either side. There were no lamps and no windows in the hallway, but a dim grey dead light, just enough to see by. He crept along the hallway, looking for signs of life and seeing none. The silence was total. Then as he approached the door at the farthest end of the passage it too opened slowly and silently. Beyond it was a small room, entirely grey, with no lamps or rugs or hangings. Thick cobwebs covered the ceiling and the walls. The grey stone hearth was cold and empty. Before it was an enormous leather chair, and in the chair sat an ancient man. He too seemed to be entirely grey, from the skin of his bald scalp and his wispy beard, to his long gown. His skeletal hands were shriveled and grey and he sat slumped in his chair, unmoving, gazing at Alec without interest or surprise. They stared at each other until Alec felt the need to break the silence.

"The door was open," he said, "so I came in. I hope you do not feel that I am an intruder."

"Few come here," answered the old man in a hoarse, papery whisper. "Why you have come?"

"I am on a journey," Alec told him. "If I am unwelcome, I can leave you and continue on my way."

"Ah, yes, the journey," said the old man. "You are fortunate, for you are near your journey's end and soon you will be free."

Alec could make nothing of this.

"Free from what?" he asked.

"Why, from this. From the choice, I made and the consequences of my choice."

"I don't understand you."

"A long time ago," said the old man, "A very long time ago indeed, I was rich and powerful and respected. My house stood on the edge of a large and prosperous town – all gone now. All gone. Then I made the acquaintance of a stranger, a newcomer to the town. He seemed to be wise and well-travelled, and I enjoyed his conversation. Enjoyed? Yes enjoyed. It is hard to remember what that felt like. So over time I came to know him well, as I thought. We discussed so many matters: the nature and purpose of life, of course. The great variety of ways in which human beings have tried to come to term with the amazing fact that we exist. And then, inevitably, we talked about death. I confessed to him that I was afraid of death, we all fear the unknown. He asked me if I would like to live forever, and I answered 'yes', without hesitation.

"Then he revealed to me that he was not himself of this world, and that he had the power to make me immortal. Of course, I didn't believe him, but I was growing older and understood that my time was drawing to a close so, half joking, I told him I would accept his offer. He warned me there would be a price to pay and – fool that I was – I told him I did not care."

"He went away soon thereafter. I felt no different, and put

the whole matter out of my thoughts. But years went by – dragged slowly by – and everyone I knew died. All the people I loved and cared for. Everyone with whom I shared memories. I felt the infirmities of old age more keenly every day. The town itself died, and the stones were salvaged for building elsewhere. No one came to visit me. They had begun to fear me. It was rumored that I was a ghost, a demon, an evil magician, and I was shunned.

"So now I linger here alone, unloved, forgotten and will do so forever. I asked for life, but not for youth or strength. At last, I understood what he meant by his warning that there was a price to be paid. And here are you, cut off while you are still so young, and yet I envy you," Alec was appalled.

"Is there no remedy?" he asked.

"None. None."

"I wish I could console you in some way," said Alec, "but I do not know how."

"There is no consolation for me," sighed the old man, "but I thank you for your compassion. I am beyond hope."

"I fear perhaps there is none for me either," said Alec. "For I am sinful man."

"We are all sinful men," replied the old man. "You must forgive yourself. Go now. Continue your journey, now that you understand it is a joyful journey."

"Perhaps I can help you," suggest Alec. "Intercede for you, when I arrive at my destination. What is your name?"

The ancient man thought for a minute.

"I don't know," he said at last. "I do not remember."

So, Alec left him and took up his path again, still faithfully accompanied by Mog. He felt grief for the old man, but comfort, almost elation for himself. Whatever he found his journey's end, he told himself, could not be as hopeless and grim as the old man's prolonged deathlessness.

Chapter 15
Mortality

On his fiftieth birthday, Roger took time from the celebrations to reflect on his life. He knew he had been exceptionally lucky. The Webster family, now his family, had been the source of all his good fortune, his prosperous trade, the sheer joy of craftmanship, and above all, his happy marriage and two fine sons. They had named the elder Simon in honor of his benefactor. The younger son was called Alan, after his own father who died when Roger was too young to remember him. He derived great pleasure from training them to the weaver's trade. His mother and Sarah had become close friends and enjoyed grandmothering together.

Today had begun with a family breakfast, and then a splendid civic dinner presided over by the mayor and alderman, with testimonials from all the leading townsfolk, praising his contribution to the prosperity and happiness of everyone. There was far too much food and drink. Only one sure note: Simon the elder had seemed not quite himself, pale and silent, eating very little. Sarah was aware of this too, and had worn a concerned expression. But, as he prepared for bed, Roger basked in the afterglow. Janet came to him and they made love. He was happy to forget his anxiety in the tender warmth of her arms.

The eastern sky was just beginning to lighten when Janet shook him awake from a profound sleep.

"It's father," she said, "something wrong."

He followed her, still cloudy with sleep, into her parents' room. Simon was lying motionless, his eyes wide and staring, his face grey. Sarah was sitting on the edge of the bed, holding his hand, weeping.

"He cannot speak," she said, "I think he has had a stroke."

"I'll get the doctor," said Roger. Hastily he dressed and ran out of the house.

"I'm sorry," said the doctor. "There's nothing to be done. He has suffered an apoplexy – a stroke. He can see you and hear you, so keep him comfortable and talk to him. He has no pain. It won't be long, I'm afraid."

Sarah sobbed on Janet's shoulder. They took turns sitting with him and talking to him, all that long day. Roger told him yet again how grateful he was, that Simon had been a true father to him. He told him that the boys, young Simon and Alan, were making great progress in the weaver's craft and the firm he had founded would continue as Webster and Sons. The light faded from his eyes towards evening, "Just as the tide was turning," said Cathy, who was a fisherman's daughter.

"Why did he have to die?" demanded young Simon. "His life was too short."

"He had a good life," answered Roger. "Good health, much love, a painless and fairly easy death. You are still too young to think about such things but as we get older our thoughts turn in that direction. We all hope when our time comes, and we know it will, the end will be like Simon's, peaceful, surrounded by the people we love and who love us."

Janet was inconsolable.

"He was my father," she sobbed. "He has always been there, it feels as if a hole opened in the world, a father-shaped hole."

Sarah was more philosophical.

"I loved him dearly," she said, "and I always will. But some day I shall be with him again, and so will dear Randall, the son we lost."

As for Nelly, she seemed to withdraw into herself, shutting herself away like an oyster. She did not weep, at least not that anyone saw, but quietly got on with her household duties, speaking to no one.

All of the worthies of the town attended Simon's funeral. Roger gave the eulogy, speaking simply from his heart, recounting yet again the story of Simon's generosity to a homeless, callow boy met by chance on the road. The mayor and the alderman gave more pompous speeches. Their wives gathered around Sarah and Janet, commiserating with sincere feeling, for they were much loved too.

Nelly had been sitting, silent and dry-eyed, but now she surprised everyone by marching purposefully to the front of the church. People stopped talking and turned to stare at her. She was very pale as she stood clenching and unclenching her hands, swallowing hard, raising a defiant chin.

"He was my father too," she said. "He took me from the orphanage. He was the only one who didn't treat me like a servant. The only one who even noticed what I was feeling or cared. I loved him. I'm going away now. They won't miss me."

Then she abruptly stepped down and marched out of the hall, staring straight ahead of her, looking at no one.

"Nelly!" cried Sarah, moving towards her. "You can't mean that. You're upset. Take a little time to think about it."

"No thank you, missus, I have thought. I'm going. Goodbye."

And she left the church.

"Well!" exclaimed Janet. "What do you make of that? After all we've done for her."

"We did treat her like a servant," conceded Sarah.

"She was a servant," returned Janet. "What did she expect? Born in shame and abandoned by her mother."

"None of that was her doing," said Roger. "Custom blamed her for something that happened before she was ever born and came to this family from nowhere, but I became a son and heir while she remained a servant."

"She never married," mused Sarah, "never even had a follower. Oh, poor Nelly."

Janet was angry.

"This is my father's funeral. We should all be thinking about him, but no, she has claimed everyone's attention."

"I wonder where she plans to go," mused Roger. "Alan, run after her. Don't let her leave without her wages, if she is determined."

Alan found her in the stable, lying on a heap of straw, a bloodied kitchen knife beside her, her wrists slashed and her blood soaking the straw. He covered her with a horse blanket, locked the stable door and returned with a heavy heart to the house.

Chapter 16
The Silver Path

Alec and Mog trudged onwards. At last, a little way ahead of him he saw another person, a small, bent man in a gown of coarse homespun and a wide-brimmed hat, plodding slowly with the aid of a stout staff. Alec soon caught up with him.

"Greeting, sir," said Alec. "Are you making the journey too?"

The man turned and looked at him from serene dark eyes. His beard was long and grizzled, his face deeply lined.

"I am a pilgrim," he said. "But I am not yet ready to complete the journey. I prepare myself by meeting others on the way and offering my help, if they want it."

He peered closely at Alec.

"You have been weeping," he said.

"I don't know where I'm going or why," Alec burst out. "1 have only just realized that 1 am dead. Is this journey some kind of purgatory, or punishment? Perhaps this is hell and I am doomed to walk here forever."

"Do you deserve punishment?" asked the pilgrim.

"Oh, yes! I have committed a grave sin."

"So do we all," sighed the pilgrim. "What is your sin?"

"I have committed the sin of fornication," confessed Alec. "I was tempted by a nymph and I sinned with her."

"Was anyone harmed?"

"Well, no, I don't think so. Except for the harm I did to my soul."

The pilgrim smiled. "My dear young man," he said, "you died too young. You missed all the experience and all the learning that most people have as they go through life. So, you need to go through it now, the good and the bad, the joy and the sorrow. Without this you could not become a whole person."

"But I was taught that what I did was evil!" protested Alec.

"More evil than murder? More evil than betrayal?"

"Well, no," Alec conceded. "Perhaps not quite so bad as that, because, as you say, no one was actually harmed."

"It was the most natural thing in the world," said the pilgrim. "If it feels wrong, you need to forgive yourself. Do you think you can do that?"

"Perhaps. In time." Alec laughed ruefully. "Or out of time. How long will it take, do you think?"

"It will take as long as it takes," said the pilgrim. "Longer for me than for you. For I was guilty of betrayal and I have set myself the doom of helping others on the journey as a penance for refusing help when it was most needed. And it will take as long as it takes. Until I feel my debt is paid in full.

"Do not despair, young man. Despair is the worst sin of all because there is no way out. Your destination draws ever closer. Look forward, not back. Perhaps we shall meet again on that distant shore. Fare you well."

The pilgrim turned away then and walked back towards the east. Alec watched his small figure diminish until it was at last lost to sight. Then with a heavy sigh he set his face once more towards the sunset and plodded forward, faithful Mog still at his side. He walked tirelessly, always towards the west across a featureless landscape. They came to a large flat rock, standing alone. On it sat a woman, small, thin, middle aged. There was such an air of grief about her that Alec could feel it too.

"Can I help you?" he asked.

"No, no one can help me, I'm beyond help now. Besides no one has ever helped me before. Why should you be any different?"

"Dear lady," said Alec "I can feel your sorrow. I am moved to pity you."

"I don't want your pity!" she exclaimed bitterly. "All I have ever had is pity. Much good has it done me."

Mog went to her and sniffed at her hands. He whimpered softly and began to lick them. She drew them away. Then Alec saw that there were deep gashes in both of her wrists although she was no longer bleeding. Then he understood.

"Do you realize where you are?" he asked her.

"No, I just found myself here. What is this place?"

"You must have been filled with despair to end your life so violently," said Alec. "Now I think you should come with me."

"Why? Where are you going?"

"I'm going into the west, to the sea."

"And where then?"

"That I do not know," admitted Alec, "I trust I shall find out when I get there."

"Who are you?"

"My name is Alec. And this is my friend and guide Mog. He wants to be your friend too."

"My name is Nelly – at least that's what they called me. I never knew my real name."

"Then come, Nelly. Let us go together to the sea. And then who knows? Another adventure."

Slowly, Nelly clambered down from her rock. Alec reached out his hand to her. She hesitated, but then grasped his hand and on they went together.

"That was a bad thing I did," she said, "to take my own life. That's a sin. I suppose I must be damned now."

"Everybody does bad things," said Alec. "We must hope to be forgiven and try to forgive ourselves. You were very unhappy, but it's over now. We must look forward not back. The pilgrim taught me that."

"What pilgrim?"

"A wise man I met along the way. A man who had learned from his mistakes and shared his knowledge with me. For I too fell into despair, and he raised me up."

They came at last to the brow of a gently sloping hill, and there before them was the sea, vast and calm, stretching to a distant, hazy horizon. The sun was sinking into the waves and staining the sea rose red. They made their way down to the shore by the light of the moon. By the time they reached it the sun was gone. The sky faded to purple and then to indigo, the darkest blue, and the sea reflected its color. The waves lapping the shore made a soft whispering sound, the only sound in that vast stillness, not a breath of wind, and no stars.

"What now?" asked Nelly. "I thought there would be a ship – or something," she added uncertainly.

"I suppose we must wait," said Alec. He sat down on the sand and Nelly sat beside him. Mog stretched himself upon the beach near them.

"I wonder how long we must wait," said Nelly presently.

"I don't know," said Alec. "All my long journey, I have not known where I was going or what would happen next. But here I am, so here I think I am supposed to be. It doesn't matter."

So, they sat quietly together in the moonlight, and waited, with no idea of time passing. At last, the moon sank lower in the western sky, and as it touched the distant horizon its reflection made a shimmering silver pathway on the surface of the sea.

Alec jumped to his feet. He seized Nelly's hand and drew her up beside him.

"You see?" he cried triumphantly. "Always, here, we are shown what to do. This pathway will lead us to the distant shore."

Nelly recoiled.

"We can't walk on water!"

"No, but it seems we can walk on moonlight. We must trust."

Nelly shrank back. "I can't," she whispered. "I'm afraid."

Mog set his front paws on the silver path and turned to look back at them.

"Go on, my good friend and guide," Alec told him. "We will trust you and follow you."

And so, the three of them stepped out on to the shimmering moonlight and walked into the west.

Chapter 17
A New World

Time passed. Young Simon and Alan learned the weaver's trade and excellent at it. Simon was the better craftsman. Alan was the salesman. Each used his particular talent to enrich the firm. Sarah and Cathy taught their young wives to dye and spin the wool. Now there were grandchildren. Roger was elected mayor for three terms before he retired and became an alderman. He continued to take an interest in the business and feared he might sometimes be offering help when it was not needed, but his sons were too fond of him to say so.

There came one day a letter from Montreal in Canada. Simon and Alan were impressed that someone so far away had heard of Webster and Sons and wanted to do business with them.

"One of us needs to go there," said Simon. "But I could not afford to be away for so long."

"Nor I," agreed Alan, "Perhaps we could invite them over here."

"Let your father go," suggested Janet. "He needs something important to do, and who better to represent us?"

Roger was delighted with the idea. To sail across the wide ocean on a great trip. To see those great towers scraping the sky. Ah, yes indeed. That would be a fine thing.

So, it was arranged that he should take the train to the great seaport and then embark on the long ocean voyage. His sons made sure he travelled in the first class, and had their agent make every arrangement for his comfort when he arrived in Montreal. So, on a fine autumn morning he set off, with much hugging and kissing and not a few tears. As the train pulled out of the station he hung out of the window and waved his hat until he was out of sight.

"Well, well," he thought. "Look at me. An orphan boy from a grey little town, sailing all the way to Canada on business. What an extraordinary life I have had! And what good fortune. It's true I have worked hard, but many work hard for little reward."

He was a happy man, contented with his life's achievement and looking forward to a serene old age, surrounded by his loving family. One final adventure, for he did not doubt that the voyage would be the last journey he would ever undertake. He dined at the captain's table and enjoyed the company of the other passenger. For some, they voyage was one of many, and they told of their experiences on earlier visits to the new world. Some were Canadians going home, who gave their impression of the old country, as they called it. There was fellowship and laughter, sometimes a little boasting, for of course everyone believed his own place was the best.

Roger enjoying strolling on the deck, watching the rolling sea and the ship's white wake. He watched early for the sun to rise behind them. And he watched late at night, when without the lights of town to get in the way to stars shone out in uncounted numbers. He observed the streak of silver mist which was the Milky Way. He saw the constant north star, and the constellation called Orion the Hunter, with the dog Sirius at his heels. He felt perfectly happy and at peace, until he remembered home and thought he ought not to be happy so far away from his loved ones. He smiled and shook his head and retired to his cabin.

On their fourth day out, as he looked out to the sea, he saw a dark cloud on the western horizon. The sky was no longer blue, but as grey as the sea, and a western wind began to blow.

"Storm coming up," said the captain, "Big'un, by the look of her."

He hurried away to give orders. Soon the masts and yards were all swarming with sailors as they reefed in the sails, while the captain put the helm about to tack into the gale. It blew harder, driving the storm clouds towards them. Through a bullhorn the captain ordered all the passengers to their cabins.

"Pack away everything that might fall or fly about the cabin," advised the steward. "You would do well to lie on your bed and hold on tight, so as not to be thrown about."

"This is a bad one, isn't it?" said Roger.

"I'm afraid so, sir, and there's always a chance you might be thrown about and injured."

"Have you been in storms at sea before?" Roger asked him.

"Oh yes, sir, many times. I'll ride it out never fear. The Nelly is a good strong vessel, very seaworthy, and the captain has many years' experience."

"The Nelly, did you say!" exclaimed Roger. "I thought the boat's name was Helen."

"So it is, sir but she's Nelly for short, so you see, to those of us who know her well."

Roger thought with a pang of the orphan Nelly whom the Websters had taken in. Poor, unhappy Nelly, to whom only old Simon had shown much kindness. Bitter, aging Nelly, who could not bear to look at life without him. An ill-omened name.

The storm closed in with astonishing speed, while the crewmen scrambled to reef in the sails. The sea heaved and roared. The ship was tossed as if it were no heavier than an eggshell, and began to take on water. Passengers screamed in panic. While the crew did their best on the commands of the bosun, the ship's officers directed the passengers to the lifeboat stations.

"Women and children first!" yelled the first officer through his bullhorn, hardly to be heard above the fury of the tempest.

"What can I do to help?" asked Roger.

"Make sure the children and the women get into the boats," said the officer. "Make sure no men get in until all of the women and children are safe. God help us, there aren't enough boats. Grab a lifebelt and make sure it's securely fastened. Better than nothing."

Roger did what he could, which it seemed to him was very little. He knew then that he was going to die this day, and resolved that his last hour would be honorable and courageous.

"I have had a good life," he told himself, "and I will have a good death."

The ship began to list to starboard, and to sink slowly as the waves pounded a hole in the hull. The boats were off, but they were tossed about like peas in a whistle, full of crying people clinging desperately to each other. The captain yelled "Abandon ship!"

The crew leapt into the water. The captain and his officers clung to the bridge. Roger chose to do the same.

"Jump, sir!" yelled the first officer.

"There's no point," Roger answered.

Instinct forced him to flail and gasp, reaching for something – anything – to cling to, but at the last the water closed over his head. Beneath the surface the sea was calm and he floated gently. To his surprise he rose again to the surface. The warm sun shone on his face and by its light he saw a shore not far off. He was a strong swimmer, and he struck out towards it. A blue sky, a beach of silver sand, and someone standing there, silhouetted against the light. A hand reached down to seize his and draw him upright. He looked into the unchanged youthful face of his boyhood friend.

"Welcome home at last, Roger," said Alec.

Afterword

My grandfather and the grandfather of my friend Mary were both born in the same small town in Scotland. Perhaps they knew each other. Mary's grandfather emigrated to Canada. Mine, orphaned at seventeen, travelled south to England, where he became a master tailor. Their two divergent roads come together again two generations later, when I met Mary in Vancouver.

Then one day in the college library, a book jumped off the shelf at me. It was an edition of the fairy tales of George McDonald. And a sort of fermentation took place. This story is the result.

It is dedicated to the two grandfathers.

I grieve for people who die young. I have known too many of them. They are deprived of the opportunity to learn and grow through experience, and become who they are meant to be. My idea of Alec's purgatory is an attempt to come to terms with this idea.

I have always been interested in the folklore of the British Isle, relics of very ancient religious beliefs and practices. The land of the dead was in the west, across the oceans, where the sun sets. During the Battle of Britain, when one of "The Few" was shot down, his comrades said he had "gone west."

The Moggy Dhu is from northeastern England: a black dog which appears when someone is about to die. I saw it once, when someone very dear to me was dying.

The Fairy song, *How beautiful they are*, was written by William Sharp (1855–1905) and first performed at the inaugural Glastonbury Festival.

Thanks are due to my editor, Paul glover, to Helen Roisum, who taught me all I know (but by no means all that she knows about spinning and weaving); to the Hazelton free range writers; to my dear Patricia, who taught me to respect spiders; and to my maternal grandparents, James and Jenny Rodger.